WOLF'S MIDLIFE BABY

MARKED OVER FORTY

MEG RIPLEY

SHIFTER NATION

Copyright © 2024 by Meg Ripley
www.authormegripley.com

All rights reserved. Printed in the United States of America. No part of this book may be used or reproduced in any manner whatsoever without written permission except in the case of brief quotations embodied in critical articles or reviews.

This book is a work of fiction. Names, characters, businesses, organizations, places, events and incidents either are the product of the author's imagination or are used fictitiously. Any resemblance to actual persons, living or dead, events, or locales is entirely coincidental.

Disclaimer

This book is intended for readers age 18 and over. It contains mature situations and language that may be objectionable to some readers.

CONTENTS

WOLF'S MIDLIFE BABY

Chapter 1	3
Chapter 2	16
Chapter 3	30
Chapter 4	43
Chapter 5	56
Chapter 6	70
Chapter 7	83
Chapter 8	98
Chapter 9	114
Chapter 10	125
Chapter 11	135
Chapter 12	151
Chapter 13	164
Chapter 14	176
Chapter 15	191
Chapter 16	203
Chapter 17	213
Epilogue	229
Dylan	241
Also by Meg Ripley	255

WOLF'S MIDLIFE BABY

1

"I'd much rather do the trust fall exercise and fall on my ass like last year." Holly Brigham had just arrived in Eugene, and so far, she wasn't enjoying it any more than she had on her previous trips. She tugged at the bottom of her swimsuit, hoping to cover more of her backside. "It's better than showing my butt to my coworkers."

"Oh, stop." Dahlia slipped her sunglasses down her nose and leaned back to get a good look. "You're too hard on yourself. At least we get to be outside having fun instead of locked in a hotel ballroom with a personnel coach and a stale lunch."

Holly sucked in a deep breath, puffing her cheeks as she let it out. "I'm not going to say that would be great, but at least I'd get to wear regular clothes."

"You're such a spoilsport!" Dahlia laughed.

It was true, at least in this case. Holly was willing to do plenty as a journalist. She knew that going the extra mile would usually make for the best story, and people didn't want to read anything that didn't captivate them. That was why she was so good at her job and had worked for the Newman Media Group for so long. She just wished she could go back to doing it at home with her laptop, but the annual meeting in Eugene, Oregon was something no employee was allowed to miss.

"Welcome, everyone! I'm so glad you're here!" As they walked to the boat ramp, a man in floral board shorts and a pink polo greeted them. Holly recognized Marshall Newman, the CEO of Newman Media Group. His brilliantly white teeth sparkled against his tan skin. "We'll have plenty of training, workshops, and news to review later, but we thought we'd kick it off with a little fun this year. What do you think?"

The crowd of about thirty or so employees around them cheered.

"Woo," Holly said dryly, not feeling the least bit enthusiastic. She could see the Willamette River just to the right, sparkling and beautiful. It was nice to look at, but that didn't mean she wanted to get in it. Even her inner bear recoiled a bit at the potential for danger. She couldn't see anything beneath the surface of the water. What was there, waiting to drag her down?

"This is Kevin, our guide on the river," Marshall continued. "He'll go over a few things so you guys know what you're doing."

Kevin, just as tan as Marshall, waved to the crowd. "Who's ready for a great time?"

"Kill me now," Holly whispered as the rest of the group cheered once again.

"What's the matter, Holly? Have you heard just how dangerous this river is?"

The voice in her ear gave her the instant sensation of slime dripping down her spine. Every year, she had to come to these meetings, and every year, she had to deal with Kyle Freeman. "I haven't, but thanks so much for that."

"It claims several lives every year, you know," Kyle continued, letting out a long breath as he looked over the river. "It's beautiful but dangerous. Kind of like you."

"Bite me." She'd tried being cordial in the past. The first year Holly had met him, she'd been happy to have someone willing to talk to her and show her around. After all, she didn't know anyone when she'd first started with the company. Unfortunately, it hadn't taken long for her to realize that Kyle was just trying to see who he could hook up with during the week they were there. It was a game for him, and she wasn't interested in playing it.

"Oh, I will if you'll give me a chance," he purred. "Really, Holly, if you get scared, just stick with me. Hey, we could tie our tubes together if you want."

"Looking at you makes me want to tie *my* tubes together," Holly hissed. "Will you shut up so I can hear what the guy is saying?" It was bad enough that she had to be in front of her coworkers in a swimsuit, but it was leagues worse if she had to deal with Kyle the whole time.

"...so if you just watch out for that, you'll be okay. Is everyone ready?"

With yet another cry of excitement, everyone hurried toward the pile of innertubes. Trepidation rose within Holly as she picked up a faded orange inflatable and followed Dahlia down the boat ramp. The water was innocuous enough when it was a few inches deep, but she could see where it dropped off just ahead.

"Here we go!" Dahlia tossed her tube in the river

and sat on it as easily as if she were getting into a recliner. She waggled her hands and feet in the water, and in a moment, she was heading off with the rest of the group.

The last thing Holly wanted was to be left behind. Dahlia made it look easy. It couldn't be that bad. People did this sort of thing all the time. She'd heard about people getting in big groups to go floating, and they found it so relaxing that they brought along a cooler full of beer to enjoy along the way. She was overthinking it. She plopped her tube down but then froze. She couldn't go face-first. Turning around, she tried to grab the handle on the side so she could sit backward. That was basically what Dahlia had done. The left side of the tube flipped straight up into the air as soon as she leaned back, threatening to dump her straight into the water.

Holly gasped, sure that she was going to die before the trip even started. Just as suddenly as things seemed to have gone wrong, the tube flattened out again.

"Easy, there." Marshall Newman himself had appeared next to her, and he held down the other handle. "I'll hold it still for you. It takes a little practice, but you'll get it."

"Uh, thanks." Her voice was shaking. No, her

whole body was shaking as she lowered herself into the river. Marshall looked so relaxed, but she braced herself against the inflated vinyl as the river took hold of her little personal raft.

"Looking good." Kyle paddled up next to her and gave her that weird upward nod guys do when they think they're being cool. "I meant all that earlier, by the way. I've done a lot of outdoor sports, and I know a thing or two. I can keep you safe out here if you just stick with me."

A foot clad in a bright pink swim shoe punched the back of his tube. "Buzz off, Kyle. You're killing the vibe."

He shot Dahlia a hateful look but then moved off to flirt with someone else.

"Thanks," Holly said as her friend pulled up. "I really don't need him buzzing around me right now."

"You're too tense," Dahlia advised, "and I mean that literally. Relax your muscles a bit."

"I feel like I'm going to fall right through this hole."

"At least no one can look at your ass now," Dahlia said with a bright smile. "Come on, honey. It's fine. If drunk college kids can do this, we can do this. If you pretend you're enjoying yourself, eventually, you will."

"Let's hope so." She forced her shoulders to relax, pulling them down so they weren't up around her ears anymore. She tried to trust a piece of plastic full of air to hold her up. It was holding everyone else up, after all. The most important thing, though, was that she didn't look down. Holly didn't want to know what was waiting for her in that water. Could she ignore it enough for the fear to go away? She doubted it.

Holly checked her senses, something she did often while working on a piece. As a long-form journalist, her writing was more than just a quick bit of information about what happened and where. It was an immersive experience, an article that would allow the reader to feel as though they'd actually been a part of something else for a while. Acknowledging all five senses in a piece and doing it artfully was one secret to success.

Holly took in the scenery around her, the trees waving breezily from the shoreline. Every now and then, she'd catch a peek at a roofline. It reminded her that she was right there in Eugene, yet in a whole different world from those going about their lives at home or work.

She inhaled deeply, her inner bear's senses coming through. The water was a tad fishy, but it wasn't bad. She picked up on coconut-scented sunscreen and the patchouli Dahlia had worn, even though it would probably get washed off.

The sound was much like a day at the beach. People were talking and laughing. A bird cried overhead. The water was different, making a trickling noise as it licked at the dirt on either side of the river instead of crashing onto the shore.

Then there was feeling. Her backside was more than cool enough, suspended in the water, but the rest of her was quite warm in the sunshine. Floating was a little like flying, and every now and again, the water would push her one way or another like a bird in the breeze.

Taste? Well, she didn't taste anything yet.

"Doing good?" Dahlia asked.

Holly allowed a small smile to cross her face. "Yeah, actually."

"You're not thinking about it like it's an article, are you?" Dahlia raised a brow over her sunglasses.

"It's a work trip, isn't it?" Holly challenged. "Besides, you told me to enjoy myself."

"Fine, girl." Dahlia laughed as she stuck her

fingers in the river and splashed a bit of water at Holly. "As long as you're happy, I'm happy."

There was nothing to do but sit there and take in all the scenery. Holly rarely found herself with that sort of chance, and she started to imagine just what kind of article she might be able to make out of this. Would Marshall even want to publish it since it happened at their annual meeting? Probably. He was pretty cool for a guy who produced several magazines, blogs, and podcasts and even owned a few local papers.

She could compare and contrast how modern people see the river as fun, but early settlers saw it more as a tool. Or she could discuss the benefits of relaxation and letting the mind wander, something that rarely happened in today's busy world. This was a modern-day adventure, and Holly knew she could tweak it into an account that would work well.

"Holly!"

She snapped her eyes open, wondering just how long she'd had them closed. That daydream had gone further than she'd thought. Alarmed, she realized that her tube was suddenly much further away from everyone else's.

"Come back over here!" Dahlia cried out, waving

her over. She and the rest of the group were all the way toward the right side of the river.

Holly, however, was toward the left. Panicking, she paddled her hands and feet, but it didn't seem to make any difference. Everyone was still shouting and waving at her, but now, she couldn't understand anything they were saying. She was just getting further and further away from them. Holly made arcing swoops in the water with her arms. Why was she so bad at this? She was from Cape Cod, after all.

Then she noticed the ripples weren't just from her movements. The calm surface of the water was breaking up into little waves, each with a crest of white at the top. Shit. She'd hit rapids! Her speed was picking up, and she careened further to the left.

What had Kevin said about this? She swore she'd heard something about it, but fucking Kyle had been boasting in her ear, and she hadn't heard any of it. There was no stopping. There was no changing direction. She couldn't do anything! Holly gripped the handles on her innertube for dear life.

"Forty-three years, and this is how it ends?"

Holly had relied on her bear instincts many times in her life, but they weren't helping right now. The beast inside her didn't know anything more about this than she did. Even if she were to shift right there and expose her secret to everyone, the current would probably just continue to carry her downstream. This was bad. This was really bad.

And then it got worse. Just ahead, she spotted a tree limb. No, it was more like a whole section of the tree that'd fallen down into the water. Smaller branches reached out from it like a net, waiting to grab her. Should she aim for it, hoping that someone could rescue her? Or should she try to paddle away? Her mind was full of fear and nothing else.

"Maybe I can push off of it," she reasoned to herself. If she could hit it just right and use it as a springboard, it would send her back toward the rest of the group. It was a long shot, but it was the only option she had.

Holly held on tight and hoped the river wouldn't take her too far to the left or right before she reached the tree. She picked up her left foot and set her heel on the tube, getting it ready for a hard kick. The raft wobbled as it sped over the rapids, and her heart had a permanent home in her throat. This was it. She was getting closer. She was going to do it.

Then, the raft tipped upside down. She clung to it as hard as she could, but it slipped from her fingers. She reached out, flailing in the water, but it was long gone. She was spinning, flying, swirling.

She heard a hollow thump, and everything turned black.

"There she is." A calm voice echoed near her head. "Her eyelids are fluttering. She's coming back to us."

Something moved under Holly's shoulder and lifted her. It turned her to the side as she coughed up disgusting river water.

It was then that she realized she was coughing that water up onto the grass. Grass! With sturdy earth beneath it! She dug her fingers into it, wanting to be sure it was real. She had that taste she'd been looking for earlier, but she wouldn't be writing about it.

"Easy, there." That voice was still there, though it'd felt like a figment of her imagination. "You're going to be okay."

She squinted up into the sunshine, but her eyes refused to focus. "What happened?"

"Your tube flipped, and you hit your head on a tree limb," the gentle voice explained. "You've got quite a bump, but I think you're going to be okay."

"Really?" Because she sure didn't feel okay. Her

bear was bursting inside her. It was surging beneath her skin all of a sudden, raging and railing even though she was now on dry land and no longer in that awful water.

"Yeah, I think so."

The sunlight behind him had been like a beacon from the clouds, but the clouds shifted and his face came into focus. Her bear went wild again as she took in his dark blue eyes, killer cheekbones, and square jaw. His wet hair dripped down onto his brow. He looked handsome, but it was his expression that got her the most. He was looking right into her eyes with genuine care and concern.

And there she was, lying in her wet swimsuit for the world to see. Maybe she should've gone for that bikini wax after all.

2

Pierce's lips tingled where they'd touched hers. He'd just been giving her mouth-to-mouth resuscitation, an exercise he'd been well trained in as a firefighter. Normally, it didn't mean anything other than saving someone's life and didn't make his wolf go berserk. It didn't make his skin have a hard time deciding whether it was cold from the river water he'd just thrown himself into or warm from the sunshine on his back. It definitely didn't make him excited to be kneeling over a woman who had bits of weeds and dirt stuck in her hair and had just coughed up half the Willamette.

But this wasn't just any woman who'd almost drowned. She was a shifter, that much he'd been able to tell right away. His inner beast had been able to sense it in her, though she wasn't like him.

She was also his mate.

"How are you feeling?" he asked, trying to force himself out of this odd state of mind. There was a procedure for everything. Any pains or other symptoms she might be having would let him know what he needed to do next.

"Like I almost drowned in the river," she responded grumpily.

He smiled. If she had enough energy to be cranky, she was probably going to be okay. "That's accurate."

"Is she all right?"

"Should I call 9-1-1?"

I am 9-1-1, Pierce thought as he looked up. He and his family hadn't been the only ones who'd come out to enjoy a nice day at Skinner Butte Park, and the commotion of the rescue had brought some onlookers. "She's fine."

"Are you sure?" A woman was holding out her cell phone. "I can call an ambulance."

His muscles tensed, knowing just what that would mean. "No, really. It's all right. I'm with the fire department, and I've got this handled. You can all go back to whatever you were doing before."

"Did you see that?" the woman with the cell phone asked her friend. "He just ran right into the river and pulled her out, carrying her in his arms! I wish I'd gotten it on video. It was like something out of a movie."

"Oh, great," the woman beneath Pierce mumbled. She wiggled around a bit, covering her body with her arms.

"Hang on." Clearly, she didn't want the audience any more than he did. He got to his feet, walked about ten yards away, and plucked a picnic blanket off the ground. He picked a few bits of grass off it before kneeling beside her and putting his hand under her shoulder. "Let's get you sitting up. This won't be so interesting, then."

"Thank you," she said as he draped it around her shoulders. She clasped the corners together, hunkered beneath it, and then squinted in confusion. "Where did you even get this?"

"It's mine. I left it here with my lunch while I was fishing with my dad and brother," he explained. As he did, he began to wonder just how far fate would go when it wanted to. They could've picked almost any spot to set up, and it just so happened to be right there.

"I'm sorry." She pressed the heel of her hand to

her forehead. "Of all the things you could've pulled out of the river, I'm sure you didn't plan to find me. Thank you, though."

"Not a problem." Damn. Even wet and dirty, she was beautiful. She was funny even when she'd almost drowned. There was no doubt that Pierce's wolf was having a thorough reaction to her. Now that he thought about it, actually, it had already started to go nuts even before he'd glanced over and seen her flailing in the water. She might not think so, but she certainly looked like the catch of a lifetime to him. "Any time."

She made a coughing sound that was probably a bit of a laugh. "Don't worry. I won't be going anywhere near inner tubes again. Ever. For the rest of my life."

The sound of splashing made Pierce look up before he could reply. A man was hurriedly walking out of the water, dragging his kayak behind him. He abandoned it on dry ground as he jogged over. Concern was etched all over his face. Unlike the other onlookers, he didn't hesitate to come immediately over. "Is she okay?"

Shit. Who was this guy? His wolf lashed out inside him, suddenly possessive and protective, though he didn't even know this woman's name. "I believe so. Do you know her?"

"I'm Kevin with Tubular River Tours." He held out his hand, but his eyes stayed focused on the woman. "She somehow got separated from the rest of us. I got over here as quickly as I could once I saw what was happening, but I never would've made it on time. I'm glad you were here."

"Yeah. Me, too." The rescue worker inside him had immediately sprung into action, but he knew that wasn't the only thing that had driven him to run into the river, swim into the rapids, and pull her free from the water.

Kevin was on his knees next to her. "What was your name again?"

"Holly." She used the edge of the blanket to sweep a drip of water off her temple. "Holly Brigham."

"Holly, right," Kevin confirmed, although Pierce doubted the guy ever really knew her name in the first place. "I'm going to have to get you to the hospital."

She instantly shook her head and pulled the blanket tighter around her. "I really don't need that. I'm fine. I promise."

But Kevin wasn't going to take no for an answer. "It's company policy, and it was in the paperwork that you signed back at the beginning of all of this. We have to go. They just need to check you out really quick."

Holly's eyes traveled up to Pierce's. Those gray-blue depths were desperate and worried, and he knew exactly why. People like them couldn't just go to the hospital. A careless nurse or doctor might not notice anything and send them on their way. Anyone who was a bit more diligent, though, who wanted to make sure they checked every little box, might find something significantly different.

"I'll take her," Pierce volunteered, giving Holly a subtle nod to show he understood. "That way, you can get back to the rest of your group and let them know she's safe."

Kevin hesitated. He glanced over his shoulder at the flotilla of brightly colored tubes where the rest of the tour was waiting.

"I'm with the local fire department, so she's in good hands," Pierce assured him.

"Is that all right with you?" Kevin asked Holly.

Though Pierce's hackles had raised when Kevin had shown up, he had to give the guy credit for making sure Holly was comfortable with the situation before he just left her to it. After all, Pierce was a stranger. Mate or not.

"Yeah, that's fine."

"Okay. I'll be getting in touch to get the hospital paperwork from you." With a sigh of uncertainty, Kevin headed back to his kayak and paddled back out to the group.

"Holy shit, this is embarrassing," Holly grumbled.

Pierce looked up at the sound of footsteps and saw that the embarrassment wasn't over for her just yet. He came from a whole family of rescue workers, and they certainly wouldn't think anything less of her for having an accident like she did, but this still wasn't an ideal time to meet her mate's relatives. "Holly, this is my dad, Rick, and my brother Hayden." He helped her to her feet, and she instantly yanked the blanket further around her shoulders so that it hung around her like a robe.

She barely lifted her eyes from the ground. "Hi."

"Looks like you've got it all under control, but is there anything we can do?" Rick offered.

Pierce looked at Holly. Now that they were standing, he could see that her head came just up to his chest. It was a detail that meant nothing in the grand scheme of things, yet he found himself enjoying that height difference. Yep. This was definitely not just an ordinary woman. "I'm just going to get her to the hospital."

The other two men nodded in understanding. "Not a problem. I'll take Dad home. Just let us know if you need anything," Hayden offered.

"Sorry I ruined your fishing trip," Holly said.

"You didn't ruin a thing, dear," Rick insisted. "Besides, you're the prettiest fish Pierce has caught all day."

"All right, Dad." There was definitely something between them, but he couldn't dare bring it up when she'd just regained consciousness. He took Holly's elbow and guided her toward the parking lot, leaving the other two behind. "It's not a long walk, but do you think you can make it? I can carry you."

"I'm good." Holly walked slowly, with her shoulders slumped and her head drooping. "I think I've been enough of a spectacle today."

"These things really do happen all the time," he assured her as they stepped onto the asphalt.

"I suppose you would know," she admitted. "I just wish it hadn't happened to me."

Though he wouldn't wish her any harm, Pierce couldn't say he completely agreed. He'd just been standing along the bank of the river, happily fishing with his dad and brother. They'd been talking about buying different bait as if it would've made any difference and how they ought to prepare the fish that night. Hayden had talked excessively for a while about his son Jack and how remarkable his recovery from his automobile accident had been, as well as how his new blended family was getting along. It'd just been a normal day, and Pierce had been content to watch the water for subtle signs of fish when his attention had immediately shifted. He didn't even know what had happened to his fishing rod because he was pretty sure he'd dropped it on the bank as he ran toward the screaming woman in the river. It had all happened so fast, and it was only now, as he opened the passenger door of his truck and helped her up inside, that he realized just how quickly he'd been running. It wasn't just the rescue worker in him. It was his soul, the part of him that knew its other half was missing.

He went around and got in the driver's seat, realizing that he had his mate right there in his vehicle, and she didn't even know his name. "I don't think I've even introduced myself. I'm Pierce Westbrook."

"Holly Brigham, although I guess you know that by now. Listen, I really appreciate you volunteering to take me to the hospital, but I can't go. I mean, I can take care of this myself, but... I don't know what I *am* going to do, but I can't do that. I don't even have my phone." She leaned her elbow on the door and tried to run her fingers through her wet hair. It was tangled, so she pulled her hand back out of the mess.

"I know. These things are much easier to handle on our own." There was no need to ask if he was right about what he'd felt in her. That shifter vibe was strong, even if it wasn't quite the same as his. "Fortunately, I've got a good connection at the local hospital. One of my packmates is a well-respected nurse in the ER. I'll give her a ring, and she'll make sure you're only around people who understand."

Holly's shoulders relaxed visibly. "Thank you. I might've been able to figure out a way to ignore that Kevin guy, but not my boss."

"Your boss?"

"That whole float trip was basically the beginning of a business meeting," she explained. "I work for Newman Media Group."

"Oh. Forgive me, but the Willamette doesn't really look like a conference room to me."

She let out a derisive snort. "Nope, not exactly. Marshall Newman has a very different outlook on things than most corporate leaders. I can respect that, especially because it means I'm mostly working remotely, but he sometimes goes a little too far outside the box."

"I see." Pierce slowly guided the truck out of the park, avoiding a group of children crossing toward playground equipment without bothering to check for traffic. The hospital wasn't all that far away, but they'd have to take a little detour first. He headed southwest, winding his way out of the heart of Eugene. He certainly didn't mind having a bit more time alone with her for now. "What exactly do you do for a living, anyway?"

"I'm a journalist," she explained, "and don't get me wrong about my job. I know I'm complaining a lot right now, but Newman is actually great to work for. I practically get free reign with my articles, and they don't even care what I wear. There are some major benefits, and I can't imagine working anywhere else, but today was a bit much for me."

"Understandably."

"I'm sure it's nothing for you since you're a firefighter. That's got to mean danger every day." She burrowed further into the blanket.

Pierce adjusted the air conditioning so that it wouldn't blow on her. "Not necessarily. There are some days, sure. Other times, we're just rescuing kittens out of trees."

She shot him a sideways glance, and for the first time, Holly didn't look half-drowned and miserable. There was a spark in her eye that sent a shiver across the underside of his skin. "You don't really do that."

"I have, actually," he admitted. "Well, it wasn't a kitten. It was a grumpy old cat who definitely knew how to use her claws, and she didn't appreciate being pulled down from her tree where she could sit and watch the birds. So maybe I *was* in a little danger that day."

"I sure hope they gave you a commendation of some sort," she said with a smile.

"No, no. They saved that for when I bravely went into an elderly gentleman's home and relit the pilot light on his water heater."

She laughed. Though it was still weak, Pierce reveled in the beautiful sound. "Did you really?"

"Actually, yes," he admitted, finding it incredibly easy to talk to her despite the fact they were still essentially strangers. "We don't normally get calls like that, but it makes more sense for us to respond to a genuine request for help instead of coming out to a structure fire later. The old guy was really grateful, too, so it was worth it. Here we are."

"Where is here?" she asked as she peered through the windshield at the woods.

"This is a small part of my pack's land. There's no reason for you to be uncomfortable. You can shift here, heal up, and then we'll head to the hospital." He got out and came around to open her door.

"Thank you." Holly moved her head in one direction and then another, looking around cautiously. Her natural shifter talents meant her body was already repairing itself somewhat, and she seemed much more lively than she'd been half an hour earlier. A shift would be the final thing to fix her up. "Um..."

"What do you need?" He lingered next to the door of the truck, knowing he'd say yes no matter what she asked.

"I, um, I know this is kind of a weird thing to ask, but do you mind keeping an eye out for me? I'm not familiar with the area, and even if it is your pack's land, I just..."

"Say no more. I'm right here with you." Pierce shut the door to the truck. He walked a short way into the woods and pulled in a deep breath. His wolf had been dying to get out ever since he'd held her body against his and carried her from the water. The earth felt comforting under his paws, and the thick coat of fur that suddenly bristled against his back quickly warmed in the sun. He shook his shoulders, letting the ripple carry all the way down to his tail. His sharp hearing picked up on a grunt as he turned and found a black bear standing behind him.

It was her. Rounded ears perched on her head amongst her dark fur. The slate color of her eyes had changed to a brown that matched the deep gold of her muzzle, a contrast to the rest of her body. Her claws were long and thick where they scraped the ground. She stretched and breathed, fully taking up the space inside her animal form. She was absolutely glorious.

She turned to him. *What do you think?*

3

"All right, my dear." Nurse Dawn Glenwood returned to the little curtained area in the ER that Holly had been occupying for the past hour. "You're good to go. I'm sorry it took so long. There was an accident out on the highway, and we had some major injuries coming in. Anyway, you should have all the paperwork you need to make everyone happy."

"Thank you." Holly accepted Dawn's packet of papers, which included all the standard information about smoking cessation and following up with her regular physician. She'd give a copy to Marshall and Kevin and then never think of this whole drowning incident again. "And thank you for the scrubs. I'll get them back to you."

"Not a problem. I couldn't have you shivering in a wet swimsuit the whole time," Dawn replied with a smile.

Holly had instantly liked the nurse the moment Pierce introduced them. She was a smart, sassy woman who didn't seem to take shit from anyone, much like Dahlia. Dawn, however, had the same secret Holly did. "I really do appreciate it."

"Sure thing. Just no more diving into the river. Doctor's orders," Dawn said with a wink as she pulled back the curtain.

Holly stepped out next to the nurse's station, clutching her paperwork and a bag that held her wet bathing suit. Her swim shoes hadn't dried out yet, and they made squelching noises as she worked her way through the ER. She headed toward the exit sign, realizing she should've asked Dawn if she could borrow a phone. All of her stuff was still back at the Tubular River Tours rental office, her phone and keys stashed safely in a locker. As she dodged past someone in a wheelchair, she realized that even if she borrowed a phone, she didn't have anyone to call. Dahlia's number was in her phone, but she didn't have it memorized. She couldn't easily use a rideshare company without her phone, either. Even if she called a cab, she had no way to pay them until she went inside the rental place and got her wallet.

She turned around to see if she could find Dawn again. Maybe she'd have some ideas.

"Holly."

His voice easily broke through the chaos of the busy emergency room. Holly turned, finding Pierce standing in the doorway as if he'd always been there.

"Are you all set?" he asked. His deep blue eyes skimmed down to her scrubs and then quickly back up.

"You're still here?" she asked, suddenly feeling breathless even though she'd been given a clean bill of health. "I thought you left."

"No. I just wanted to step out and let you have some privacy for all that." He gestured vaguely toward the curtained partitions behind her. "I wasn't just going to leave you."

"That's really kind of you." She walked with him out into the waiting room. The automatic doors slid open, blasting them with a hot gust of air as they stepped into the circular driveway where vehicles could bring patients right up to the building. "I was just trying to figure out how I was going to get out of here."

"Complimentary service of the Pierce Westbrook

Cab Company, of course." He once again swung open his passenger door for her and even held out his hand to help her up.

Her inner bear went wild as his strong but gentle grip easily guided her into the seat. A hot firefighter who was also a nice guy *and* a gentleman? It was almost too good to be true, even though she was experiencing it all personally. Too bad she had to almost drown to find him and that he lived on the opposite side of the country.

"Where can I take you?" he asked as he started up the engine.

Why was it so intimate just to be in a vehicle with him? It felt like they were the only two people in the world and that there was far less distance between them than the wide truck cab allowed. She studied his profile for a moment, enjoying the slope of his nose, and then reminded herself that she was on a work trip. "The tube rental place. I'd look up the address for you, but I have to get there first to get my phone."

"No problem. I know where it is." Pierce easily backed the truck out of its spot and headed out onto the road. "I think I've got most of the town memorized at this point."

"I suppose you would. There's no time to sit

down and play with navigation when you've got to put a fire out." Despite everything she'd been through, her mind suddenly started playing with Pierce's job as an article. He'd joked about helping an older man with his pilot light, but he'd done just as much good with that little task as if he'd extinguished a fully engulfed structure. His job was truly about community, a far more selfless position than most people had. There were plenty of senses to explore, too. The crackle of flames, the smell of smoke, the feeling of heat...

"Tell me more about what you do," Pierce said, interrupting her thoughts. "I know you said you're a journalist, but do you write about anything specifically?"

"Lots of things, really. For me, it's more about finding the stories no one realizes are there. For instance, a big event that brings a lot of visitors to a small town would be the sort of thing that any basic news outlet would talk about. I'd want to see it from behind the scenes, from the perspective of a small business owner who'd been thinking about closing their doors for good before the sudden influx of tourists. It's even better when that business owner is the kind of person who invites you up to their apartment above the store to have a cup of tea and shows you the old advertisements from when her grandfather opened the place."

Pierce smiled. "That sounds rewarding."

"It can be. Sometimes, it's hard to find the right story. Plenty seem like they'll be something, but then they turn out to be duds. That's life, though."

"I can't argue with that. What else do you have going on besides writing? You know, besides tubing."

She laughed. "I'll never live that down." Was he trying to ask if she was seeing anyone? She wondered the same thing about him. The guy was probably about her age, early forties or so. She didn't see a ring on his finger, but that didn't mean much. Not everyone went straight to the altar the moment they met someone, and she had no doubt the local women were coming up with ways to set their kitchens on fire so that he'd come bursting through the door.

"Well, we're here. I'll come in with you in case they need any information from me since that Kevin guy wasn't too sure about me taking you to the hospital." He parked the truck and got out.

Holly didn't think they had any reason to speak with him, but since she found that she liked his company, she didn't argue. She stopped at the little locker she'd rented first, fetching her keys, her original bag of clothes, and her phone. There were too many notifications to fit on the screen, and they'd collapsed in on themselves so that they only listed the number of missed phone calls and text messages.

Marshall Newman was checking in on her. *Give me a call as soon as you have a chance. I just want to make sure you're all right.*

There were a few messages from Dahlia as well. *Girl! You gave me the scare of a lifetime! Looks like some hunky dude rescued you, though, so maybe you planned it? I'll see you back at the cottage unless you make other plans with him.*

Holly rolled her eyes, knowing Dahlia would absolutely flip once she heard it all. Then she frowned, seeing some messages from Kyle.

You'll have to stick with me for the rest of the trip so I can keep you safe. I tried to get to you to pull you out of the water myself, but those rapids were crazy.

There was more to his text, but she stuffed her phone in her bag.

"Didn't miss anything too important, did you?" Pierce asked.

"Just someone asking about my car's extended warranty," she cracked. Kyle was a whole subject of his own, and she wasn't going to dive into that right now. They stepped up to the window where day-trippers could rent tubes, kayaks, and life vests. "Hi, I'm Holly Brigham. I was with Kevin's group earlier, and—"

"Oh, that was you!" The young guy behind the counter stared at her with wide eyes. "You okay? Everyone was talking about that!"

A flush of red crept over her cheeks. "I'm fine now." She didn't doubt that they'd all had plenty to say about it, and that would probably continue tomorrow when she went to the next phase of their annual meeting. She handed him one of the forms Dawn had given her. "Kevin wanted paperwork to show that I went to the hospital."

"Right. Cool. I'll make sure he gets it. I hope your experience doesn't keep you from using us again."

"We'll just have to see," she said with a smile before they turned and headed back for the door. She hoped she never stepped foot anywhere near Tubular River Tours again, even though none of this had really been their fault. She should've been paying more attention, both before she got into the river and after.

Pierce had happened to park right next to her rental, so they headed in the same direction as they stepped out into the parking lot. "Listen, you've had a bit of a rough day. I know you've had a chance to heal up, but I'm happy to follow you to your place if you like. Just to make sure you get there okay. You did hit your head, so I'm not sure how you feel about driving."

Oh. Damn. As Holly looked up at him, she could feel her entire existence pulling her toward him. She'd found plenty of men attractive before, and she'd made several stabs at relationships, but nothing had ever quite worked out. This was far more than she'd ever felt, and Holly knew it wasn't just because he'd saved her life. He was so handsome and sweet, and she was so tempted. She realized, though, that she hadn't told him the most important thing about herself as they'd been chatting. "I think I should let you know something about me."

"If it's that you're a different species, I already know that," he cracked. "I don't know exactly how it would work, but I'm not opposed to it."

"It's not that!" she laughed, "although I guess that would be new territory for both of us. I'm not from around here. I'm just here for our annual meeting, but I'm actually from Cape Cod, Massachusetts. I'm just here for a few days." Holly paused and licked her lips, wishing all of this had happened differently. She didn't know how it could've been better, considering they lived on two completely separate coasts, but anything that didn't make this so difficult and awkward would be preferable. "I just...I just thought I should say something before things went any further."

Pierce put a hand in his pocket but didn't back away or tell her to forget the whole thing. He thought about it for a second, staring off into the distance over the river, and then looked down at her. "I should've put that together earlier, but thank you." He paused, looking like he wanted to say something else, but his lips didn't move.

"I should probably get going. I've wasted enough of your time as it is." Not that she wanted to leave him. She liked spending time with him, even if they were just driving around Eugene in his truck. It was simple, but that was all that was required. How could it ever go anywhere, though? She stepped past him toward her car.

His fingertips brushed her elbow. "Holly?"

Her heart must've found a jump rope somewhere, considering the way it was bouncing in her chest. "Yeah?"

"I know you won't be staying, but would you like to see the town from a local's perspective while you're here?" His eyes blazed into hers, brilliant and alluring. "I could pick you up tomorrow night and show you some great places, including a few that never make it onto the tourist maps. It might be kind of fun."

Holly knew she shouldn't. She had a few days in Eugene for the meeting, and then she'd be flying back home. Going on a date with a stranger would throw a wrench into everything. The logical part of her brain reminded her of just how quickly things could get complicated. Her bear didn't really care how complicated things got as long as she got to spend more time with Pierce. None of it really made sense, and there was no answer that seemed quite right. "Sure," came out of her lips despite all of that.

"Great. I'm looking forward to it. Where are you staying?"

"My friend and I are sharing an Airbnb." She grabbed her phone so she could give him the address and, consequently, exchange numbers. A thrill ran through her as she thought about what she was doing. Holly wasn't the sort who went to a new town and found a handsome stranger to spend an evening with. In fact, she'd fully planned to spend her evenings there either working on her writing or perhaps knocking back a few glasses of wine with

Dahlia. This just wasn't the sort of thing that happened to her, yet there it was, unraveling right before her eyes.

"Sounds good," he said, looking up from his cell phone. Their eyes locked.

She felt it, knowing he must, too. The pull between them had been working at them all afternoon, stretching and straining at them like a strong magnet. It was finally getting its way, and there was nothing she could do to stop it. Hell, she didn't even think she wanted to stop it. The space between them closed, and their lips met. Pierce's lips lingered on hers for a long moment, but he didn't try to push it further. He stepped back. "Can I pick you up at eight?"

You damn well better after that. "Yeah. That'd be perfect. I'll see you then." Holly got in her car before she could make any other wild decisions. Her hands shook as she tried to figure out which key she was supposed to put in the ignition, but then she remembered it had a push button start. Hoping that Pierce wasn't watching, she fired up the engine on her rental car. Her bear didn't want to leave him, but Holly knew she needed some distance to calm the hell down.

She sped toward the little cottage she and Dahlia

had found online, glad that at least it wasn't too far away and she knew how to get there. She didn't need to get lost and have yet another disaster, not today. It was hard to concentrate on traffic in a whole new city when her bear wanted only to think of that kiss. It was the first she'd had in a long time. It wasn't some big dramatic display, but it sent radiating waves of warmth and excitement through her body. His hand had grazed her hip in the moment, hinting there was more he'd like to do.

Holly enjoyed her quiet life in Cape Cod, but changing coasts would mean changing everything.

4

"Is that what you're wearing?"

"What's wrong with it?" Holly looked down at her fitted V-neck tee, jeans, and favorite boots. It was a simple outfit, but that was how she liked them.

Dahlia folded her arms. "You look like you're going grocery shopping."

"Is that really so bad? Besides, anything I wear right now is going to be better than the drowned rat look I had going on when he first met me. I still can't believe the poor guy saw me in my swimsuit."

"All the more reason to give him the razzle-dazzle," Dahlia insisted. "What else did you bring?"

"Not much." Holly sat on the edge of her bed while Dahlia looked through the closet. "Just some comfy clothes for anything outside and a few things for the meetings."

"You can't just go to the other side of the country and not plan for at least the *chance* that you'll need a nicer outfit," Dahlia chastised, flicking through the few clothes that Holly had hung up since she'd arrived. "Do you have any heels?"

"Just the ones I was born with," Holly cracked.

"Maybe instead of going out on a date with this Pierce guy, you and I should go shopping." Dahlia retreated from Holly's room and into her own across the hall.

Following her, Holly shook her head. "I've tried. Have you seen the monstrosities they try to pass off as women's fashion these days? With puffed sleeves, ruffles, and giant floral prints? I'm well past the stage when my mother used to stuff me into fancy dresses to go see my grandparents."

"It's not *that* bad. You just have to know how to find the right things. I saw a navy skirt in your closet. Try that with this cream top." Holly shoved a sleeveless shirt at her, the soft material bunching in her fingers.

"And the shoes?" Holly challenged.

Dahlia scrunched her face, accentuating her freckles. "I'll let you have your boots. You said he's going to show you around, so there's a chance you could be walking."

As Holly went back to her room to change, Dahlia hung out in the hallway. "A handsome stranger on a work trip. That sounds like something out of a chick flick."

"Maybe, but I'm trying really hard not to think about it like that." Holly pulled on the top, but her bra was the wrong color and showed right through. She took everything off to start over again.

"Why not? Let your hair down. Have some fun! You work hard, and you're a grown woman. You deserve it."

"Okay, sure." Holly had to concede on that point. She wiggled the skirt on, and even she had to admit it looked pretty cute together. "I just don't want to get myself too excited about the whole thing. He lives on the West Coast, and I live on the East Coast. We've both got jobs and lives and all that. There's just no way it would work, even if he is—"

"Even if he's what?" Dahlia pressed. "Hot? Polite? An actual good guy who risked his life to save yours?"

Even if he's my mate, she told herself. "Yeah. All of that." Holly put her boots back on and took a look in the mirror. She hated to admit it, but Dahlia had been right. This was a much better outfit.

"Here." When she stepped out of the bedroom, Dahlia practically attacked her with a pair of silver dangly earrings. "You need to accessorize!"

Holly took them from her, but as soon as she stepped back in front of the mirror, she heard the sound of a truck pulling up outside. Her hands instantly began shaking too hard to even come close to hitting the holes in her ears. "I think that's him."

"Oh, yay!" Dahlia ran to the front door.

Looking at her reflection, Holly wondered just what the hell she was about to do. Pierce seemed like a hell of a guy so far, the kind she could wax poetic about if she wanted to. She'd resisted because she knew it would only pull her further into this connection with him that her bear was so set on. She'd explained her situation, so she couldn't give herself too much guilt over the idea of leading him on, but it still just didn't feel right. Why go out with him if they both knew it was going to end, anyway? Her suitcase peeked at her in the mirror from around the side of the bed, reminding her just how quickly the clock was ticking.

"So you're the hero who pulled my lovely little

Holly out of the river," Dahlia was gushing in the front room. "That was very impressive."

"I was just doing what anyone else would do," he replied, his voice a deep rumble through the cottage that set Holly's bear off all over again.

Dahlia laughed. "You probably didn't notice because you were too busy diving into the rapids, but everyone else pretty much just sat around like idiots. Anyway, I'm trying to thank you for saving Holly's life."

"I was happy to do it."

"I bet you were."

Holly knew she'd better get out there before Dahlia started giving him a safe sex talk. Exhaling a slow breath, she stepped into the living room.

Pierce instantly looked up at her. His name was perfect for him, since his eyes pierced straight into her soul. He captured her with little more than a glance, and suddenly, Holly felt delighted to be dressed up a little. Her earrings tinkled softly, and she was suddenly aware of the way the fabric of her skirt fell across her hips.

"You look beautiful."

"Thank you."

Dahlia pressed her lips together as she looked back and forth from one to the other. "You two kids have a good time. Drive safely and make sure you stay out too late!" She winked at Holly.

Grabbing her purse, Holly ushered Pierce toward the door. She made a face at Dahlia just before she closed the door. "Sorry about that," she said as they entered his truck. "Dahlia is very enthusiastic and actively tries to rub that off on me."

"You're not enthusiastic?" he challenged, raising one brow as he backed out of the driveway with expert ease.

"I am about some things," she replied, letting the implications hang in the air. Holly was far more excited to be with Pierce than she should be. It was just a simple date, a nice little tour of the area that he'd offered. She could even try to convince herself that he'd offered it out of pity if it weren't for the way her bear was reacting. It felt warm and cozy being there in his vehicle with him, pleased to finally be in close proximity once again. It reminded her of just how big the bed in the little rented cottage was when she slept in it alone, just like her bed at home. It churned inside her as she studied the hard, muscular lines of his arm and the way his jeans fit around his thigh.

"Anything you're particularly *not* enthusiastic

about so I can make sure we avoid it? Other than anything to do with the river, of course."

She had to laugh. "You're never going to let that go, are you?"

"Not for a while," he admitted with a grin.

"Fine. Then categorically, I'd have to say I'm not enthusiastic about team-building exercises."

He flicked on his turn signal. "That's very specific."

"I know, but that's what I've been doing all day. These annual meetings are a good way to distribute information about the company as a whole and talk about future goals, but Marshall has this idealistic dream about his employees being best friends. That's why we all had to float down the river yesterday, and that's also why we had to spend today doing things like splitting into groups and finding one thing that every person in that group has in common. Or one person has to be blindfolded while another guides them through an obstacle course just by talking to them."

"Does any of this make you a better writer? Or a better employee?"

"Please, bring that challenge to my boss! Marshall would find a way to say it does, though. I can't blame the guy for trying, but getting a bunch of introverted, creative types to interact and get to know each other is quite the stretch."

"Dahlia doesn't seem very introverted," he noted.

"No," Holly snorted. "There are a few exceptions."

He parked the truck and quickly came around to open her door for her, even though she'd fully recovered and was more than capable of doing it herself. "Looks like we've come on a good day."

The light breeze carried delicious scents to her as soon as her feet touched the asphalt, and her mouth began to water. "Wow. What is that?"

"Look over there." He pointed to a gathering of food carts near an outdoor market. "Are you hungry?"

"Sure." They walked together through the little circle of food carts, which offered everything from fish tacos to kebobs to loaded fries. Some were offering breakfast food, even though it was dinner time. "I don't know how I'm going to pick."

"That's always a problem around here. There are just too many good options. Let's see what they've got here."

When she had a fat vegetarian burrito in her hand and Pierce had picked up a Monte Cristo sandwich, he led her back out onto the sidewalk. "I've got an idea for a great place to take you, but I figured we could walk there and just take in the sights on the way."

"It's so pretty here," she noted as she dabbed a bit of guacamole off the side of her mouth. "I'm ashamed to admit that I've never really ventured out much the other times I've been here."

"You've been missing out. There are some great outdoor markets, especially on the weekends, plus beer gardens and wineries. Not that we don't have chain stores, but there are tons of locally-owned places, too. Any of that is a lot more exciting than having a scavenger hunt with your coworkers."

Holly laughed. "You know, we actually did do that last year. It probably wasn't the worst thing, at least. What about you? I take it they don't have you do that kind of training with the fire department?"

"No. They're more concerned with all the boring stuff like CPR and first aid. You've got to try this." Pierce held out half of his sandwich.

She touched his hand as she bit off the corner. It was just a bite of food while they stood in the middle of the sidewalk, yet it felt incredibly intimate. Holly took a quick step back as she nodded in approval. "That's delicious. Do you want a bite of mine?"

"Sure."

She watched with intrigue as his teeth sank into the tortilla. It shouldn't be sexy. It really shouldn't, yet Holly couldn't help but think she'd much prefer him taking a bite out of her.

"I'll be honest," he said when he'd swallowed. "That tastes much better than I thought anything vegetarian would."

"Definitely." It was a small thing to agree on, yet it pleased her to know they had something in common. If anyone had asked Holly what an ideal date would be like, she wouldn't have thought about checking a random gathering of food carts. Walking around town, just enjoying the buildings and trees and seeing how happy the people looked was much better than dinner and a movie. It was real life, a beautiful blend of businesses and residences side by side, and it made her want to know more about the area. What was the history behind all of this? Was there a reason for the unusual architecture of that building? How many businesses had inhabited it over the years, and what were their stories? Then, there was the band playing live on the street corner, happily churning out music for anyone to hear. What would be the future of that little girl who danced so freely to their songs? Would she be a musician one day? The sights, smells, and sounds filled her, and she loved it.

She also noticed something else about the area, even though she hadn't specifically been looking for it. "There are a lot of people like us here, aren't there?"

He smiled again, that killer grin that made her lose herself in the way his lips moved over his teeth. "Plenty, yes."

The image of him in his other form came to her mind, the glorious wolf that had so easily flowed out of him. He was confident and comfortable in his beast, and it was a view to enjoy. It also made her question all over again just what fate had in mind when it threw the two of them together. "I get the feeling much more of them are like you than me."

He shrugged casually. "Yeah, I think so. We're not really all that different, though. Are we?"

Not as different as they could be, since they shared a secret they had to keep safe from the rest of the world. It was a difference she wouldn't mind exploring if they didn't already have a much bigger difference that came as more of a challenge. Pierce was part of this beautiful community. She was part of her own back in Cape Cod. Right now, that felt like far more of an obstacle between them than the species of their shifter forms. "Maybe not."

"Let's turn the corner here. There's a great place I want to show you, and I think it showcases everything that Eugene has to offer. Or at least a lot of it." He gestured to the right.

"Like what?"

"Good drinks and good music, all for people like you and me."

They jogged across the street and up to a plain brick building. 'Selene's' had been painted in curling white letters directly on the façade. A marquee board over a solid black door advertised the lineup of bands for the night. Directly in front of that black door stood a large man with his arms folded across his chest. Instantly, Holly began to question herself for going out with a stranger. She belonged at a library or café, not a rock club with heavy music pumping through the thick walls and a bouncer staring them down.

But Pierce walked straight up to him without any hesitation. "Hey, Max. Anything good happening tonight?"

The sour look on the bouncer's face instantly turned to a friendly one. "Oh, yeah. Rex and Lori are both working tonight. They've got good bands and a good special, so the place is hopping. I think you'll find a lot of familiar faces, although I see you've brought a new one with you."

"Max, this is Holly. She's visiting from Massachusetts, so I thought I'd show off the best place in Eugene."

The dark-haired man smiled kindly at her as he grabbed the doorknob behind him. "Very nice to meet you. Watch your step on the way in, and don't get too close to the stage tonight unless you like a rougher crowd. The restrooms are in the back corner behind the bar, and make sure you don't tip the bartender. He's an ass."

"He's his brother," Pierce explained.

Max ignored him, continuing to address Holly. "If this guy gives you any trouble, just let me know." He opened the door for her with a flourish, letting pounding rock music escape onto the sidewalk.

Charmed, excited, and a little nervous, Holly stepped into the dark interior.

5

It was a short hallway that bent around to the left and soon opened up to reveal the main floor of the club. A small but professional stage stood on the right, and the crowd around it throbbed in time to the music. Chairs and tables began to take over the floor as it neared a large, carved oak bar. The walls were painted black, but band posters and other memorabilia blotted the darkness. Just as Max had promised, the patrons were having a great time whether they were dancing, drinking, or laughing with each other over the din.

Pierce guided her over to the bar, where a woman with butterscotch brown hair was expertly mixing drinks as she continued taking orders. She smiled when she saw Pierce walking up. "Hey there, hot stuff. Haven't seen you in here for a while."

"I've been busy," Pierce replied. "Lori, this is Holly. She's in from out of town."

"Oooh, a newcomer! Then let me get you started with a Barrelman. It's my trademark drink, and the first one is on the house. Just don't tell Rex." She snagged two lowball glasses and scooped some ice into a shaker.

"Don't tell Rex *what*?" The man working at the other end of the bar instantly lifted his head, hearing the comment despite the chaos in the club.

Given the mischievous look on Lori's face, she'd meant for him to. "That I'm giving all the drinks away for free tonight."

"I knew I never should've hired you." Rex, a burly man with wide shoulders, came just close enough to snap a towel at her ass.

"Do that again, and I'll get my revenge when we get home," Lori promised with a sly grin.

"You can't take these two anywhere, not even to their own club," Pierce told Holly. He picked up the drinks Lori had swiftly served them and led her over to a small table in the back corner. "Do you remember Dawn, the nurse you met at the hospital?"

"Of course."

"Rex and Max are her brothers. Rex is our Alpha, and Lori is his mate. I guess you could say we're all pretty tightly knit. Actually, there's their other brother right now." He lifted his hand to greet a blond man who'd just stepped away from the bar. When he came over, Pierce made the introductions.

"You're definitely a long way from home," Brody said as he shook Holly's hand. "There are a lot of great souvenir shops around here, but the best one is mine. If you like tattoos, I'll give you a good deal on one before you leave."

"I'll think about that," Holly promised, realizing as she said it that she genuinely meant it. The night had been a simple one so far, but it was making her fall in love with this town and the people in it. Maybe Dahlia was right and she really did just need to let her hair down a bit more. Her friend would die of shock if she came back to the cottage with a tattoo to commemorate the trip.

"I know it's a little loud, but this really is one of the best places to come for music. Have you heard of the band Wildwood?"

"Of course. Hasn't everyone?" Holly wouldn't consider herself to be a huge music buff, but it was hard to turn on the radio without catching one of their hits. She paused as she realized just what Pierce was trying to tell her. "Don't tell me they play here..."

"This is their home base these days, now that Declan moved back home," Pierce explained.

She smiled at him. "I guess you're going to tell me he's part of your pack, too." It was easy enough to say it out loud since the music was blaring.

"Maybe." He took a sip of his drink, his eyes sparkling over the rim of his glass.

"Are you trying to impress me?" she dared to ask.

"Maybe." Pierce put his drink down and leaned toward her across the table. "Is it working?"

"Maybe," she replied with a laugh.

Pierce glanced around the room. "I'll be right back. Are you okay on your own for a second?"

"I think I can handle it." She enjoyed the view as he got up and walked toward the restrooms. Pierce's job obviously kept him fit, and he filled out a pair of jeans nicely.

"Holly!"

Holly was instantly filled with revulsion. "What are you doing here, Kyle?"

"I should be asking you the same thing!" He threw himself into Pierce's seat and turned to look around the room before he leaned closer, his breath smelling of whiskey. "Who's the guy?"

"What? Why?" The question caught her completely off-guard.

"Listen, Holly. The people around here are weird. Really weird." He rested his elbows on the table and looked firmly into her eyes. "You need to watch yourself."

She leveled her gaze at him. "He's the one who pulled me out of the river, if you must know. I think if he had any bad intentions toward me, he would've just let me drown."

Kyle shook his head. "I'm telling you, something's different about these people."

"I don't recall you ever mentioning it before," she noted, "and we've been coming here for annual meetings for quite some time now."

"I know. I just wasn't paying attention." He glanced around the room again. "I don't know what it is yet, but there's definitely something unusual happening here. The people around here aren't like you and I."

They were far more like her than he could ever imagine. They might not be bears, but Holly was feeling more and more comfortable as she understood just how many shifters surrounded her. Maybe a dark nightclub wasn't typically her bag, but it was nice not to have to keep her secret held so tightly against her chest. "I'm fitting in just fine, thank you."

He didn't seem to hear her. His jaw was set, and his eyes were constantly scanning the place. He'd squared his shoulders, looking like he was trying to play the protagonist in an action movie. "I can keep you safe, Holly. I'll take you back to your place. Let's go right now while we have the chance."

She scraped her chair back as he reached for her hand. "Just what the hell do you think you're doing?"

"I told you. I'm keeping you safe."

Holly shook her head, suddenly understanding exactly what was going on. Kyle happened to see her hanging out with the guy who'd saved her from the river. He was jealous, especially since he'd been trying to get in her pants for years, so he'd come up with a hero act of his own. It wasn't going to work. "I'm fine, Kyle. Really. I'll see you at the meeting tomorrow."

"But—"

"Really," she insisted. They'd have to continue working together in some capacity, so she didn't want to be rude, but she didn't want to ruin her night with Pierce, either. "I'm fine. I'll see you tomorrow."

A deep furrow creased his brow, and for a

moment, he looked like he wasn't going to take no for an answer. "Just be careful, okay?"

"I will." The only danger right now was the risk of losing her heart to a man she couldn't have. He appeared through the crowd just after Kyle left, making her heart jump all over again.

"I hope I didn't keep you waiting too long," he said as he returned to his seat.

"Not at all. I was just wondering, how long have you been with the fire department?" Her irritation with Kyle was easily forgotten as she sank into the comfort of Pierce. As they continued to talk, the club seemed to fall away around her. She hardly heard the music any longer, concentrating only on the sound of his voice and the way his mouth moved when he spoke. She noted the gentle twitch of his finger every now and then and the way he rubbed his thumb through the condensation on his glass.

"Do you want to dance?" he asked, standing up and holding out his hand.

A bit of the fantasy faded as reality set in. "I'm not much of a dancer."

"Neither am I, but no one's going to be looking." As soon as she set her hand in his, he brought her down toward the crowd around the stage.

The music crashed into her ears again, flooding

her body and making her move. No, it wasn't just the music. It was *him*. Being so close to him made her feel as if she'd been missing out on something for a long time, like a part of herself had finally been regained. His hand brushed against hers, then her hip. The lights sparkled and her skin tingled. She was drunk but not on alcohol. With a happy sigh that only she could hear, she followed Dahlia's advice and truly let herself go. She didn't care about who was looking or how good of a dancer she might be. She only cared about being close to her mate.

They moved through several songs until a final crescendo indicated the end of the set. Pierce captured her in his arms as they stumbled through the crowd, laughing and sweating. "Do you want to come back to my place?"

She sucked in a breath, but there was only one answer that could possibly be right. "Yes."

They escaped from the noise and chaos of the club, running out the door and hurrying through town to Pierce's truck. Holly laughed as he pulled her along by the hand, both of them eager to find a private moment together. Even without that privacy, he found a way to show his desire for her when they paused at a crosswalk and waited for traffic. Her hand still clasped in his, he brought it up and pressed his lips gently to the back of her fingers.

In the truck, Holly still felt that complete lack of inhibition. She boldly lifted the center console out of the way and scooted over to sit directly next to him, pressing her thigh against his. She trailed her fingers along the back of his head, relishing the soft feel of the hairs that'd been cut close, and kissed his neck.

"You're making it difficult to drive." It obviously wasn't a complaint, since his right hand cupped her knee and slowly moved upward, pushing the fabric of her skirt out of the way as he massaged up the length of her leg.

"Did you want me to stop?" she teased, already knowing the answer.

He gripped her thigh harder, his need for her radiating out from his fingertips. "Definitely not."

"Good." This wasn't like her. She was shy and reserved, waiting for a man to approach her instead of overtly showing him how she felt. It was different with Pierce, and Holly started to think maybe this actually *was* like her. She just needed Pierce to come along and bring it out. Perhaps finding a mate completed her in more ways than she realized, even if they wouldn't be able to stay together.

At his apartment, they barely got the door shut behind them before they were in each other's arms. Holly pressed her hands against his chest and spread them wide, exploring his strong pecs and shoulders. A thrill ran up her spine and she grazed her fingers down his arms, enjoying the firm muscles under his skin.

Another hardness was making itself apparent as Pierce gripped her hips and held her tightly against him. The bulge at the front of his jeans grew as he bent to kiss her neck, nipping at her jaw, and his hands slid around and down, cupping her buttocks. He scrunched her skirt with his fingers until he'd moved enough of the material away to find her panties. By this point, his lips were on hers again and his deep groan of pleasure echoed in her mouth.

Holly let out a groan herself. There was no greater excitement than knowing she turned him on. Her senses were overwhelmed as she tried to take it all in and memorize it, wanting to lock this moment away and keep it forever. The woody scent of his cologne, mingling with his soap underneath. The sight of his eyes as they drank her in, so full of desire that she could hardly see the blue of his irises. The sounds he made emanated through her, a groan or a sigh every time he found a curve of her body that he hadn't gotten to know yet. And taste? There was no shortage of that as their tongues danced and entwined or as she kissed the salty sheen from his skin.

Then there was the feel of him, a sensation so pleasurable, Holly hardly knew how to describe it. His hands brought her to life everywhere they roamed, making her suddenly aware of every dimension of her body. She could never write about it, not this. She wanted to keep it all to herself.

Pierce let go of the back of her skirt, but only so he could run his fingers under the waistband and push it down off her hips. The cute little cream top turned into little more than a scrap of fabric in his big hands as he pulled it up over her head. Another moan of appreciation escaped his lips now that he could see her only in her bra and panties. He bent to kiss the fullness of her breasts where they peeked out from the soft cups. His hands encircled her ribcage and moved around behind her back, expertly releasing the clasp at the back and setting her free.

Holly shivered at the sudden rush of air against her skin, making her nipples harden. Pierce quickly made up for it by pulling one into the heat of his mouth. Her core was already beginning to tighten, and they hadn't even made it out of the entryway yet. She kicked her way out of her boots as she reached for the hem of his shirt.

Leaving his own shoes behind, Pierce began guiding them down the hall, though neither of them was willing to let go of the other. He staggered as she pulled his shirt over his head and tossed it back the way they'd come. He caught himself against the wall with one hand, the other tightening around her waist to keep her close.

They stumbled through the bedroom door as she scrabbled with the button fly of his jeans, slowly revealing him inch by inch. That left them with only their underwear, and the wild possession that'd overtaken her was more than she could bear. She ripped the last remains of the barrier between them as they tumbled onto the bed.

He was hard and ready for her, throbbing against her as she put her knees on either side of his hips. Holly felt that aching need echoing inside her, a desire that could only be sated by one thing. She lowered herself onto him, gasping at the size of him and just how good it felt. The world spun around her as she rode him, reveling in the depth and intimacy of this new connection. His hands roved over her body, worshipping her like a fine marble carving as he held the weight of her breasts then cupped her backside. She ground harder against him as she felt herself getting closer. Pierce grabbed her hips, moving both of their bodies with his sheer strength. Holly cried out as the tension inside her uncoiled. Wave after wave crashed over her, each one feeding the next until they seemed as though they'd never end. When they finally let go of her, she collapsed on top of him.

"Come here." Pierce lifted her off of him and laid her back on the pillow. He braced his feet beneath him as he positioned himself between her legs, pulling her up onto his lap and sinking into her once again. He held her against his chest as he thrust his hips faster and faster.

Holly still felt the aftershocks moving through her. Watching him pulse against her, with his stomach rippling and a look of pure ecstasy on his face, quickly made those aftershocks come together to create another earthquake inside her body. She wrapped her legs around him, her thighs shivering and shaking. She thrashed back against the sheets as the pleasure overtook her. Pierce held on tightly as he reached his peak, burying his length inside her as all that they'd been working toward released.

As they lay together on the rumpled blankets,

Holly's bear couldn't remember ever feeling quite so satisfied, as though nothing in the world outside of this room mattered. She felt herself glowing with pleasure, wondering how she could ever go back to normal life after this. Her body was already craving another round with him.

A loud chirping erupted through the room.

"Sorry." Pierce launched himself to the edge of the bed, leaning down to grab his jeans off the floor. "I can't really ignore that, not with my job. Hello?"

She had to admire that. He was a man who people called when they needed help. He'd certainly shown up to help her, a favor she'd owe him for forever. Holly adjusted the sheet over her naked body and enjoyed the sight of him, propped up on his elbow and turned away from her as he listened to the other end of the line. She hadn't yet had the chance to enjoy just how good his backside looked without his jeans on.

Her enjoyment stopped when he sat up straight, every muscle in his body tensed. Something was wrong.

"I'll be right there." He hung up and turned to face her. "My dad's house is on fire."

6

Pierce's feet hit the floor before he'd even finished flinging the sheets aside. His heart pounded as he grabbed his boxers and pulled them on. He'd joined the fire department not only because he wanted to help his community but also because he enjoyed the thrill of danger. This wasn't the same. Not this time.

"I'll get out of your way, but let me know if there's anything I can do," Holly asked as she slid out of bed. Not as familiar with the room as he was, she found the switch on the bedside lamp and turned it on.

"Out of my way?" he asked, pulling his shirt over his head. Where had his damn pants gone? Ah, there. "You're not in my way, and you don't even have your rental car here."

"I'll just get an Uber or something," she said. Her voice shook, though she was trying to sound casual as she got dressed alongside him.

"No." He would worry far more about her if she had to find her own way back to her Airbnb, which would make dealing with this fire call even harder. Pierce wouldn't mind if she stayed at his place, but then he'd feel like he was abandoning her without her rental. His mind raced through options and quickly landed on the right one. "Come with me."

"Are you sure?" She wiggled her hips as she tugged her skirt back on.

"Yes," both his wolf and his human answered. He already knew what she was to him, but wanting to have her by his side at a moment of such disaster only confirmed it. This wasn't the time to worry about a mate or the implications of bringing her with him, and he let himself fly along on instincts for the moment. "I'm sure."

She got dressed just as quickly as he did and hurried out the door with him, waiting to tie her boots until she got in the truck. "How bad of a fire is it?"

He gripped the wheel as he flew out to the edge

of town. He could still hear the dispatcher's voice echoing in his head. *We got a call. It's your dad's house.* "Bad enough that they sent the whole team out before they called me, so it's not just a stove burner that got out of control."

"I'm sorry," she whispered.

He felt her genuine concern. He needed it, but it only made his situation more difficult. Holly was amazing. She was smart and cute, a demure writer who looked at the world with wide eyes. Tonight, she'd also shown that she could set herself free, her body moving alongside his both at the club and in bed. Now, she was comforting and caring. How unfair was it that she'd only be there for a few more days?

As he rounded the corner, his heart sank into the pit of his stomach. The column of smoke and steam that rose from the house had turned pale, the lights of the fire engines that surrounded it flickering in the misty air. Where once there had stood a beautiful house, a place Pierce would always think of as home, there now only remained a hollowed-out shell. The skeletonized framing supported part of the back wall where the kitchen had been. Hunks of melted metal and plastic that were formerly appliances still lurked there, recognizable only because of their shape and placement to each other. Most of the roof had caved in, and debris had scattered everywhere. "Holy shit."

"Oh, no." Holly put her hand over her mouth.

With the driveway full of emergency vehicles, Pierce parked on the lawn. He stepped onto the grass that Rick had always been so meticulous about. His father would've thrown a fit over tire tracks through his precious greenery, but it didn't matter now. Water squelched up out of the dirt, runoff from the fire department's efforts to save their chief's home. He spotted a familiar figure standing on the walkway that led up to where the front door used to be and slowly moved toward them.

Holly slipped her fingers between his. "Would you like me to come with you?"

He tightened his grip in answer, walking through a nightmare to where his father stood watching the smoldering remains of the home. "What happened?" His heart had worked its way back up and into his throat, and the words barely strangled out around it.

Rick turned and laid a hand on his shoulder. "Electrical fire." His eyes dodged to the side, noticing Holly. "Hello again, young lady. I'm glad to see you've recovered."

"Yes, thank you. I'm—I'm so sorry for your loss."

Tears glimmered in his eyes as he crossed his arms in front of his chest and turned his gaze back to the subject at hand. "Thank you. I have to say, I've never liked it when we've seen this happen to someone else. It's even harder when it happens to you. Someone else loses their home, and you start thinking about how to help them get a new roof over their head, some clothes, and a couch to sit on. When it's you, you don't even know where to start."

Hayden came around the corner of the house, still clad in his gear. He stripped off his helmet and chucked it on the ground. "Son of a bitch. We got here as fast as we could, Dad."

"You and I both know that sometimes it doesn't matter."

"Still." Hayden did a double take as he noticed Holly and gave her a polite nod. "I'm sorry my brother dragged you along for this. You must think Eugene is nothing but natural disasters at this point."

"That's all right." Holly's hand slipped out of Pierce's and tucked around his waist. "I'm sorry that it's happened."

Pierce returned the embrace, settling his arm along her back and cupping her hip in his hand.

Sadness moved through him like a whole new beast that inhabited his body. The porch where he and Hayden used to wait for the bus, fighting over who got to sit next to Joanna Murphy, was now just a hunk of concrete, barely visible under the half-burned pieces of wood that'd fallen from the porch roof. On the second floor, all the way to the left, a few shards of glass remained from the window of his childhood bedroom. He used to watch their little neighborhood from there, sitting on his bed and dreaming of what his life would be like someday. He'd sat on that bed and even dreamed of finding a mate, especially as he'd reached high school and some of his friends were already meeting the people they were supposed to be with. Pierce had wondered when it would happen for him, knowing it would be the start of something incredible.

He'd found her, but this wasn't exactly the happy ending he'd hoped for. He was about to lose her within a matter of days, and it didn't feel so different from the house burning down. When Holly was gone, he would feel just as hollow and damaged as the remains of the home before him.

"Damn thing is, I had an appointment with an electrician scheduled for next week," Rick said quietly.

"What was happening? Was something acting up?" Hayden asked.

Rick shook his head. "No. Not a thing. Nothing was any different than it had been for years. I was just getting frustrated that there was only one electrical socket on the outside of the house, so I was going to have him put in another one. The place was old, and I thought I'd have him check everything else out while he was here. I'm sorry, boys."

"Don't apologize, Dad." Knowing that his father felt bad about the whole thing only made it harder to bear. "It could've happened today, tomorrow, or three months from now."

"Yeah, I know. And we can all justify it any way we want to, but I still feel terrible about it. There were a lot of memories in that place, both in my mind and in the physical things. Your mother had put together those baby books, and she had a box for each of you up in the attic with some of the things from your childhood. There was the doorway where I measured you each summer."

"I was always taller," Hayden said, giving Pierce a sad smile.

"Not always," Pierce replied. "There was that one summer when everyone called you my little brother."

"I know the material things shouldn't matter," Rick went on. "Even when they're sentimental, they're just things. But, well, it sucks."

"I know, Dad." Hayden put his arm around Rick's shoulders. "It's the people that really matter, though. That's something I thought about a lot after Jack had his accident. Pierce and I are just glad to know you're all right."

Pierce glanced down at Holly. Her head was tipped back, the light from the fire engines flickering over the various angles of her face. Yes. Hayden was right. It was the people that mattered. It broke his heart to know that all the memories from his childhood home were gone, but what was he doing to create new ones? What memories would he be missing out on when Holly returned to Cape Cod? She was right there next to him, her back warm against the inside of his arm, the feeling of her body still fresh on his, yet he already missed her. His wolf was crumbling under the grief of the house and of her.

Holly's eyes slowly traced over the scene before her, and Pierce had to wonder what she was thinking. She was a writer. She'd told him how she liked to look for the story that no one else noticed. When they'd been at Selene's, he'd asked her more about her work. He'd been fascinated to hear how she liked to pick things apart into the different senses and how she wanted to completely recreate a world to drop a reader straight into it. Was she doing that now? What story could there be other than one of loss and sadness?

Rick rubbed his hand over his face. "I know. And you're right. I just need to quit moping and start thinking about what I need to do. I've got to call the insurance agent. I guess I might as well get all the utilities turned off because they'll charge me a minimum even if there's not a single lightbulb on."

Pierce turned his mind back to the real matter at hand. He could feel sorry for himself knowing that Holly wouldn't stay, but it wouldn't change the fact that they had a lot to deal with now that the house was gone. "You know we'll help you out with all of that, Dad. And you should take some time off of work, too."

"You don't think I will?" Rick asked.

"We know you won't," Hayden replied.

"Can you blame me? I think I'll need to work to distract me from all of this." Their father gestured helplessly at the wreckage.

Just as Pierce was hoping Holly would be around long enough to distract him for a while, she slipped out from under his arm. She moved over to the side, where a row of oak trees separated their property from the neighbor's. The trunks of the trees still remained, but the leaves and limbs closest to the home were singed badly. She hunted through their remnants for a moment until she found a sturdy stick. With her new tool in hand, Holly walked over to the remains of the home and poked the stick down into the ashes.

Pierce moved to her side, cautiously watching what was left of the home. "The house was always sturdy, but it's not right now. It could be dangerous."

She didn't look up at him, focused only on digging in the ashes. "But look."

He looked down at his feet, where his boots stood on the scraps of his life, and caught a glimpse of something shiny. He stepped back and used the toe of his boot to move a half-burned board out of the way. The movement uncovered the rest of what Holly had been excavating, and he let out a breath that collapsed his lungs. "No way."

"What are you two doing?" Hayden asked.

"Give me your gloves," Pierce commanded.

"What?" But he stepped forward and handed them over.

Pierce pulled them on, knowing everything there

would still be deceptively hot. It would take a long time for anything to cool down enough to be touched. If Holly's discovery was what he thought it was, he wasn't going to wait. He bent down and lifted the corner of a picture frame. The wood was badly damaged, burned and then soaked. The photo inside was mostly preserved between two pieces of glass, with only the corners taking on some discoloration. "Look what Holly found."

"I'll be." Rick leaned in to see, and he didn't fight the tear that ran down his cheek. "I haven't been able to find that photo for years. I actually went looking for it a few months ago, on what would've been your mother's birthday. It must've slipped behind some furniture or something."

The Westwood men took a long moment to study the scene in the picture. Rick, young and proud with his arm around his wife. Linda, beautiful with her hair curled around her face and her chin lifted. The couple stood in front of their home, with freshly bloomed flowers standing out against the siding. Their boys were just in front of them on the steps. Hayden was twelve, right in the middle of that awkward stage just before his teen years hit. Pierce stood next to him, still boyish and goofy at ten.

There had been other family photos, Pierce

knew. There were even times when they'd gone to the trouble of getting dressed up and going into a studio, but this one had always been Rick's favorite.

"That was a good year," Rick said, just as Pierce knew he would. "Thank you, Holly. I've lost a lot tonight, but you've given me back a little piece of it. It's like a miracle, and I needed that."

Sadness moved across her face. "You're welcome."

Rick sighed. "Well, it's late. I have a lot to do, but I can't do any of it until the morning. I think I'll head over to the packhouse for the night. I'm sure Joan and Lori can set me up with a room, and their beds are far more comfortable than what we have at the firehouse, anyway."

"You don't have to do that, Dad," Hayden began, but Rick stopped him with a wave of his hand.

"I've already thought about it. Your house is full, and I can't exactly stay here unless I want to sleep under the stars. I'm not too keen on camping these days. It's the only thing that makes sense."

"Just come stay at my place," Pierce insisted. "I know it's not huge, but I do have an extra bedroom."

"I know, but..." Rick hesitated as he glanced in Holly's direction. She'd stepped slightly away from the group of men to give them their privacy. "I don't want to be in the way."

It was kind of him to consider Pierce when he was the one suffering so much. The truth was, Pierce would probably be better off if he didn't give himself much more of a chance to get any closer to Holly. Everything indicated she was his mate, but that didn't mean they could work out the distance between them. And what if they tried? He'd already seen Hayden go through the process of marrying someone that he thought was right, only to suffer when it all came crumbling down. It hurt him, but it would only hurt worse if he tried to force it. "As long as you're not counting your sit-ups at five in the morning, I think we'll be fine."

7

"You're in big trouble, young lady."

Holly smiled at the voice hissing in her ear. "Oh, look. They have cheese Danish. My favorite."

"Give me some of that." Dahlia held out her plate, her eyes widening as she looked at the flaky crust of the pastry. "Okay. I'm a smidge less upset with you now, and I'll be a smidge less than that once we get some coffee, but you're still in trouble."

"What did I do?" Holly asked with a smile, though she knew precisely what was happening.

Dahlia followed her down the buffet table, which featured every delicious snack and treat Eugene had to offer. Marshall Newman was big on supporting small businesses. She put on her best mom voice: "Coming in after midnight, young lady, without so much as a holler to let me know you were home safe! Why, I've got a mind not to let you see that boy again!"

Holly laughed. "Don't worry, Ma. I probably won't."

"Now, hold on a second." Dahlia had been reaching for a plate of fruit but paused and gave Holly a stern look. "By my calculations, you still have one more night left in Eugene. Granted, we have a bit more of this bullshit to get through, but you've got enough free time to squeeze in another dinner or movie or *whatever* it is the two of you might've been doing." Dahlia waggled her eyebrows at Holly.

"Technically, sure, but it's not like it can go anywhere." She reminded herself of this constantly, knowing how easy it would be to fool herself into believing that fate and love would be enough to make things work. If that were true, she would've already found someone long before now.

"Ugh." Dahlia made a deep noise of annoyance in her throat. "I keep telling you, it doesn't have to *go* anywhere. It could just be a really nice time, a chance to relax and enjoy yourself before you head home."

"Who says I don't enjoy myself at home?" Holly contended.

"Okay, fine, but I think you and I have different definitions of enjoyment." Dahlia loaded her plate with fruit and a few more pastries before the two of them headed off to a table in the cafeteria at Newman Media Group's headquarters. "And anyway, neither of you must be looking for this to go anywhere if you didn't even stay the whole night at his place."

Holly stirred a generous amount of oat creamer into her coffee. "You want to know all the details?"

"Every. Grisly. One."

"Fine. He literally ate right out of my hand."

"What?" That made even Dahlia sit back in her chair and pay attention.

Holly shrugged. "He wanted to try my burrito."

Dahlia narrowed her eyes. "You're impossible."

"Yes, but it actually was really nice." She detailed their impromptu meal from the food carts, the walk around town, and their time at Selene's. It'd been so perfect. She'd had guys take her out for fancy meals at snooty restaurants where the menu was all in French, but her time with Pierce had been so much more enjoyable. The rock club was unlike anything she'd ever been to. Not even when she'd been in college had she ventured into a place like that, but she felt so safe and happy with Pierce. "You'd be very proud of me if you'd seen me out there on that dance floor. Not for my dancing skills, necessarily, but for the fact that I actually danced at all."

"And then?" There went Dahlia's eyebrows again.

"We went back to his place." She had nothing to hide or be ashamed of.

"Don't leave me hanging," her friend warned. "Knowing you, going back to his place could mean doing the nasty or it could mean organizing his bookshelves."

"No bookshelves were involved unless we happened to knock something off one accidentally, and I was too busy to notice," Holly replied, her body feeling warm all over again. Pierce knew just how to touch her. He made her feel so desirable, so sexy. She'd be basking in that afterglow for a very long time.

"Okay, now we're talking!" Dahlia realized she was starting to get loud and giggled.

Holly bit into her Danish and chewed thoughtfully. "Then there was the part about his father's house burning to the ground."

"What?" Dahlia clapped her hand over her mouth as several coworkers turned their way.

"Yep. He got a call while we were lying in bed, and we rushed off to the scene. It was horrible."

Holly had relived every moment she and Pierce had shared together in bed, but she wished she could erase the rest of the night from her mind. "It was the house he and his brother grew up in, and everything they had was completely gone. I don't think I've seen anything quite like that firsthand."

Dahlia leaned across the table. "Wait. He took you with him?"

"Don't start reading into that," Holly warned. "It was just the most convenient thing to do since I didn't have a vehicle. It was a matter of timing, that's all."

Wasn't it? Because even though Pierce needed to rush off to be with his family, Holly could've figured out a way home. She could've called a cab—an option that was actually feasible since she had her purse with her, unlike when Pierce had pulled her from the river—or she even could've called Dahlia. It would've worked out. But looking into it too much would lead her down a path of disappointment all over again. She and Pierce liked each other. That much was evident. Fate certainly had big ideas about them, considering the telepathic link between them when they'd had a few moments to be in their animal forms together. There was no getting around the physical distance between their homes or even the fact that they were different species. How would that work? Every time she rolled it all around in her head, the situation became more jumbled and complicated.

"If you say so." Dahlia polished off her pastry and washed it down with some coffee. "I'm just saying I don't think any guy I've dated has ever invited me to a family emergency."

"All right, folks!" Marshall Newman clapped his hands to get everyone's attention. "I hope you've all enjoyed your break. Even though we're here to have fun, we still need to sit down and recover from it every now and then."

A few people laughed politely.

"Erica is passing out index cards, each with a symbol on it," Marshall continued. "We're going to use these to split everyone up into smaller, random groups. If you're a triangle, you're going to be staying right here in the cafeteria with me. Stars will be heading down the hall to the conference room. Squares will go outside into the courtyard, and circles will go upstairs."

Holly took the little slip of paper from Erica and flipped it over to show Dahlia. "I'm a square."

"You sure are," Dahlia agreed with a smile. "Looks like I'm a star, baby."

Once they'd cleaned up their table, Holly made her way toward the doors. They were inset into a large glass wall that showed off the beauty of the courtyard, a lush space full of flowers and other indigenous plants. There was no telling what kind of team-building torture awaited her out there, but for once, she wasn't too concerned. She'd get through the day, and then she'd be heading back home. Going back to everyday life was exactly what she needed right now.

Lorelei, the HR director, was waiting for them at the center of the courtyard. "Welcome, everyone! I know we've done a lot of great activities so far this week to help us get to know each other. I hope that by asking questions and exploring what you have in common, you've all become much more comfortable with your coworkers. Our goal for this week is to have you all enter as coworkers and leave as friends."

Holly pressed her lips together to keep from making a smart remark.

"First, we're going to become the human knot! The goal of this game is to improve our strategy and communication skills, and we'll probably get to know each other a little better along the way! I want everyone to get into a circle. Make it nice and tight, shoulder to shoulder. Just like that. Perfect. Now, everyone, put your left hand out. Take the hand of someone on the opposite side of the circle. Make sure they're not your immediate neighbor."

A hand quickly clasped hers, squeezing tightly. She looked up and found Kyle on the other side of the circle. Fantastic.

"Now, everyone, put your right hand in and do the same thing, but you can't take the hand of the same person who's already holding your left hand!" Lorelei chirped.

Well, good. She might be stuck with Kyle on one side, but that was it.

"Wonderful! Your goal is to untangle yourselves without letting go. You'll form a perfect circle when you're done. Remember to use each other's names and think about how to work with everyone to solve the problem. There's no time limit!"

Kyle yanked her close and leaned in. "I need to talk to you."

"No, you just need to duck under that guy's arm," she replied, pointing with her chin.

They churned through several rotations before he had a chance to get close again. "I'm working on a big story."

"Good for you. Now turn to the left." She watched the churning knot of people, wondering how something that made them all rub up against each other could possibly be okay in today's corporate culture. No one was objecting, though. In fact, they were laughing and chatting as they tried to sort themselves out.

He pulled closer to her once again, even though it didn't help their progress. "I'm glad to see you made it out of that club last night."

"I appreciate your concern," she said, nearly gritting her teeth in annoyance. "I can take care of myself, though."

While some people on the other side of the group worked through a particularly dense section of the knot, Kyle took his chance to continue. "Most of the time, maybe, but you got lucky."

She sure did and allowed herself a small smile as she thought about it.

Holly had never been fond of these exercises, but she suddenly found herself interested in achieving their goal. The sooner they untangled themselves, the sooner she could distance herself from Kyle. She turned to the other person she was holding hands with, a photographer named Dennis. "I think if you duck over that way, the next guy can spin to the left."

Dennis nodded. "Sounds good to me. By the way, I really enjoyed that piece you did a couple of months ago about the coffee shop. It was neat to see all the history from the point of view of the building. Great stuff."

"Thank you. I appreciate that. It took a lot of research and interviews to get it all together, but I really enjoyed it."

"It's important to enjoy your work," Dennis agreed as they churned through several more people, ducking and twisting. "Me, I can't imagine doing anything other than looking at life through a lens. There's so much to see in the world, and it gets overwhelming. I like distilling that down, pointing the finger at something really specific. If you don't mind the comparison, I think you and I have a bit in common."

"I think you're right," she agreed. "If you find yourself in New England, we should work together sometime."

Kyle grumbled at her as the crowd moved back in the other direction. "You need to be working with me. If you want angles and perspectives, I've got something that will knock your socks off."

With one final twist, the knot turned into a circle once again.

"Yes!" Lorelei cheered. "Awesome job!"

Though Kyle had started on the other side of the

circle, he was standing next to her now. Holly gave him a flippant look. "I think I'll keep my socks on, thanks."

She managed to stay away from him for the next few exercises, but she couldn't avoid him completely once the day wrapped up. With a bag of Newman Media Group swag over her arm as she walked outside to her rental car, Kyle once again caught up with her.

"Holly, I need you to hear me out. No, just listen," he insisted when she opened her mouth.

She shut it again, figuring that maybe if he got it all out, he'd finally leave her alone.

"We all know you have amazing skills in immersive writing. And we also know I'm Newman's best investigative reporter. If we team up on an article, we could both be up for a Noomy. Marshall's personal pick might not mean much to the rest of the world, but it's a step toward being nominated for an Edward R. Murrow Award or maybe even a Pulitzer!"

Working with Kyle was the very last thing she wanted to do. He was talented, but she had a feeling he was setting his sights a bit too high.

"Now, here's the really important part." Kyle grabbed her elbow and pulled her to a stop between two SUVs. He glanced around, making sure no one was nearby. "You remember that I told you there's something funny about the people around here, right?"

Holly was pretty sure there was something funny about him, but she stuck to her policy of hearing him out so he'd shut up. "Yes."

"I think I've got it figured out." He leaned close, his cologne too strong. "I spent a bit of time in that club last night. People don't think anyone can hear them when there's loud music playing, but I've got a great ear. I kept hearing them saying weird things like they were going out for a run. I figured it was a code phrase for drug deals or something. I mean, no one goes out for a run after they've been dancing and drinking at a rock club. Right?"

Her throat had gone dry. This couldn't really be happening, could it? "Sure, but you never know—"

"So I followed a few of them," he continued, his brows furrowing down over his dark eyes. "Holly, what I'm about to tell you is absolutely wild. Understand that I'm telling you—and only you—because I think you're the only person I can trust with this information."

Or because he wanted to work with her or somehow thought it might get her into bed with him. Holly waited on tenterhooks, terrified of what he might say next.

"They're not—" He looked around again and then lowered his voice so that it was barely above a whisper. "They're not human. These guys left the club on foot, and I followed them at a distance. For a bit I thought maybe I was mistaken, but then they got to some of the parkland near the river. And Holly, I shit you not: They changed into *wolves.*"

She'd always known it could happen. The wrong person at the wrong time would get too careless with their secret, and someone else would be just nosey enough to see it. Her mind reeled, and her body threatened to lose balance. What could she do? "Are you sure?"

"I've never been more sure of anything in my life." Kyle had given her his arrogant, macho attitude many times before, and it was rare that she saw any shred of authenticity in his personality. It was there now, though. He wasn't laid-back Kyle, who hoped to get laid on a company trip. He was Kyle Freeman, investigative journalist, a man on a mission to expose a massive story. "I didn't have a drop of alcohol in that club. I was completely aware and sober. I'm talking teeth and fur and tails. Everything.

I have no doubt I can recreate what I saw by spending time in the right places."

He straightened but still had a hold of her elbow. His face was hard and serious. "You believe me." It was a statement, not a question.

How could she not? Though not a wolf, she was one of the very subjects Kyle wanted to pursue. "Yeah," she managed.

Kyle gave a slight nod. "I'm going to stay in Eugene for a few days longer and pursue this. I'm not telling anyone at work about it, not even Marshall himself. I have to keep it under wraps until I'm ready to bring it out into the spotlight, so as far as anyone else is concerned, I'm just taking vacation time. What do you say? Are you with me?"

It was an impossible situation. Kyle was a pain in her ass every year, and she couldn't wait to leave him behind. But if she did, he stood a chance of being much more than a pain in the ass to thousands of people. If he were successful and did a good enough job that people could actually believe him instead of laughing him out of the newsroom, it would change everything. Not just here in Eugene, and not just here in America. The entire human civilization would experience a massive paradigm shift they probably couldn't handle. Holly wanted to believe that Kyle wasn't capable of making waves that big, but what if he was? There were many ifs, which was precisely what scared her.

"Sure," she finally said, knowing she had no choice. She had to stay, and she had to work on this project with Kyle, but not for the reasons he hoped. Holly had to completely botch the story and keep it under wraps. That was the very antithesis of what she was all about, but the risk was too great. "I'm in."

8

"Sorry there isn't very much closet space," Pierce said as Rick stepped out of the guest bedroom. "I've just been using it for extra storage, but I can take those boxes and put them somewhere else for a while. I should be able to get them out of your way in a couple of days."

"Don't worry about it," his father insisted. "And aren't I the one who should be apologizing to you? Encroaching on your home and everything?"

Pierce resisted the urge to roll his eyes. "You're not encroaching. I invited you. Besides, we're family. This is just how it works."

"Yeah. I guess so. Listen, is it all right if I put my shampoo and conditioner in the shower?" He thumbed over his shoulder at the bathroom at the end of the hall.

"C'mon, Dad. Of course, it is. I was just telling you I'll get things out of your way so you'll have a place for everything." He knew all this was only coming out because his dad felt so lost and out of place. Pierce had never thought his apartment was big, but maybe he'd been taking even that tiny amount of square footage for granted all this time. "And really, I'm going to get those boxes out of your way."

Rick had retrieved his shampoo and conditioner from the dresser and put them on the edge of the tub. "It isn't like I've got much to put in the closet right now. I'm lucky enough to have kept some extra clothes at the fire station, but I'll have to go shopping sometime soon."

"Right." Pierce felt bad all over again. He hadn't meant to remind Rick that he was left with nothing after the fire, but it was a topic that seemed impossible to avoid. "I can go with you sometime next week."

Rick sat on the couch as they returned to the living room but didn't lean back into the cushion. He sat with his elbows braced on his knees, looking ready to spring forward at any moment. He hadn't really been comfortable since he arrived. "Jessica has already told me she's taking me. Then Paige and Ellie jumped in on it as soon as they realized it meant a trip to the mall. I don't know how much shopping I'll actually get done, but that's all right. Hayden's girls are sure a hoot."

The timer on the kitchen stove went off, and Pierce stepped in to grab the pizza from the oven. "I can't say you're in for a culinary adventure while staying here at Château Pierce, but I promise you won't go hungry. You want to grab a couple of sodas while I slice this?"

"Sure." They arranged themselves on the recliners in the living room, their plates loaded with pizza and cold sodas on the table between them. "I suppose I've been technically living the bachelor life for the last ten years with your mother gone, but it feels a little more authentic in an apartment eating frozen pizza."

"Is it really so bad?" Pierce asked with a smile. He found himself smiling around his father almost all the time lately, trying to find anything that would keep him in good spirits. He felt so bad for him. Yes, it was sad for Pierce, too. No doubt Hayden was grieving in his own way. But both of them had grown up and moved out. It had to be much harder for

Rick. "I've always got junk food in the freezer, cold beers and sodas in the fridge, and far more streaming services than any one man could possibly need."

"Oh, that's just fine for me. I suppose you think it's fine for you, but I have to wonder what your girl Holly thinks about the whole thing." Rick picked up the toppings that'd fallen onto his plate and put them back onto his pizza.

Pierce nearly choked on a pepperoni slice, but he should've expected the subject to come up eventually. Hayden and Rick had both been around when he'd pulled her from the water. They'd been gentlemanly enough not to ask questions when she showed up on his arm after the fire, but they weren't dumb. There had to be something going on for her to be there with him in the middle of the night. "I don't know that I'd call her my girl," he began.

Rick blotted his lips with a paper towel and then folded it into the palm of his hand. "She seems very nice."

It was an open door into the rest of the conversation. Looking back, Pierce realized his father had mastered that a long time ago. He'd never come right out with demanding questions when he wanted to know what was happening in his sons' lives. Instead, he'd casually bring the subject up and then just let it hang in the air. His patience had always been much greater than that of his boys.

That was when they were younger, though. "Yeah. She is."

"Sort of has that shy sweetness about her," Rick continued. "At least, that's how it seems to me, but I can't say I've been around her under the best circumstances."

Pierce was hesitant to say too much. Holly was amazing, but his relationship with her—if it could even be called that—was complicated. "That's true, but she's pretty great in any circumstance, from what I've been able to tell. She's got a quick wit."

He'd enjoyed more than just her wit a few nights earlier. Holly was warm and sexy. She'd seemed to come alive when they'd gone to Selene's and were around their own people. As the confidence grew in her, so did his attraction. Pierce hadn't really intended to bring her out onto the dance floor. He'd just wanted to show her around and make sure she had a good time while she was there, but the music and the atmosphere had completely taken him over. He was fairly certain the same thing had happened to her. Now, thinking about it without the dull thump of bass behind them, Pierce knew it wasn't the music or the club at all. It was what the two of them had together, a connection that was hard to explain or describe. Something was fascinating about watching the lights from the stage move over her face, casting her skin in tones of blues and purples. His eyes had narrowed in on her hips and shoulders as she moved, her body twisting and writhing in a rhythm that his body already understood. They proved that all over again when they'd gone back to his place and fallen into bed together, where the dance had continued without any music to blame.

"She certainly impressed me by pulling that old photo out of the ashes." Rick opened his soda, the hiss of the carbonation cutting into the air. "When you've been a firefighter as long as I have, you know how people tend to react. They just stand around and gape or completely freak out. She didn't do any of that. She started looking around, really studying the scene in front of her. I'm sure that's why she found that photo, and I really am grateful for it."

"I'll tell her," Pierce promised as he polished off his first slice of pizza. He'd have to figure out when he'd see her again, though, or maybe if he would at all. It didn't seem right to spend such a magical night with her and then just let her fly back to the other side of the country. It might as well be the other side of the world.

Rick pulled in a deep breath and let it out slowly. "I didn't need that photograph to remember what it was like to be with a good woman. It's the sort of thing that stays with you that you don't really ever forget. Holly seems like one of them."

He was trying to push the door further open to get Pierce to come out and say what was happening between the two of them. Of course, there wasn't much to report. "Maybe." Pierce could feel Rick's eyes on him, studying him.

"You don't really think I don't know, do you?" the older man asked softly. When Pierce looked up, he continued. "I'm no dummy, son. I saw the way the two of you looked at each other, even at the scene of the house fire. I saw that sense of longing, of belonging, but not quite figuring out how to do it. I've been there, Pierce. It's been a long time, but like I said, you don't forget."

Pierce frowned at his soda and wished it was a beer, but he knew no amount of alcohol could distract him from the way he felt about Holly. "She's special. I'll give you that."

"Hoohoo, I'd say," Rick replied, sounding more enthusiastic than he had since the night of the fire.

"It was no accident that you pulled that girl out of the river. You shouldn't wait too long if something's going on between you. Our time is precious, and we have to take advantage of it."

Time was even more precious than his father realized. "It's not like it really matters. She's only here on a business trip, and she'll be going back home soon."

"It always matters, son. Even the smallest relationships—the ones that don't work out and that we can laugh about twenty years down the line—matter. It's all part of who we are."

"You're pretty philosophical tonight," Pierce noted. He knew a lot of that was because his father had lost his home. That gave him cause to get a bit reflective and start thinking about life. He'd done the same thing when their mother had died. "I'm not going to say you're wrong, but Holly lives all the way on the East Coast. I think she said she leaves tomorrow."

Rick's gray brows lowered. "Then why are you here sitting on your ass? If there's a chance something might work out, you need to go to her. Even if you just wined and dined—and whatever else—with her, you ought to at least be gentleman enough to see her off."

He was right. The damn old man was right again, just as he often was about everything else. It'd always pissed Pierce off when he was a teenager and was so convinced he knew more than his father, only to find out he didn't know a thing at all. He was forty-four now, so it wasn't like he should have many lessons left to learn. But as he chomped down on his pizza, he knew he still had to figure out how to navigate some things. "I wouldn't mind a chance to say goodbye," he admitted.

His father gave him an approving nod.

When he'd finished eating, Pierce changed into a nicer shirt, combed his hair, and brushed his teeth. He caught himself in the mirror, wondering what he was doing all this for. She was going to leave. She wouldn't care if he had a hair out of place or if the pocket tee he'd been wearing had a dot of pizza grease on the hem, yet he couldn't help himself. She was his mate, whether they'd be staying together or not. He'd at least leave her with one last good impression.

"I'm heading out," he announced when he returned to the living room. "You behave yourself. No wild parties. The neighbors will complain, so don't think I won't hear about it if you try."

"No promises," Rick said with a smile.

Pierce headed back to Holly's Airbnb with his heart in his throat. He'd get to say goodbye, but the thought of doing so was much easier to handle than the reality of it. It just wasn't right to know that his mate had been right there with him and was now about to leave. He tried to think of what he might say to her, but everything seemed wrong. Tension built in his muscles as he grew closer to her place, creating knots in his shoulders.

Even his legs were cramping as he came up the porch steps and rang the bell. He was there to say goodbye, to let her go. His wolf twisted and raged inside him, telling him he had to think of something else. He had to find some way to make this work, but the more logical side of his brain knew that was impossible.

The door swung open to reveal a tall redhead. Dahlia's catlike eyes swept up and down his body before she turned to call over her shoulder. "Holly! There's a handsome firefighter at the door, so it must be for you! Come on in." This last part was directed at him, and she stepped aside to wave him into the foyer living room just as Holly emerged from her bedroom.

"Pierce." Her dark hair had been pulled back into a ponytail. She wore a loose T-shirt and knit shorts, and she nervously plucked at the hem of them. "I wasn't expecting you."

"I know," he admitted. "I'm sorry to just drop by, but I know you said you'd be going soon."

"We're finally freed from the doldrums of overly enthusiastic meetings about cooperation, learning, and happy work environments," Dahlia confirmed as she stepped into the kitchen. "Can I get you anything to drink?"

"No, thank you." His throat was dry, but he wasn't even sure he had the strength to hold a glass as he stood there looking at Holly. His wolf was going wild, and it would take every ounce of effort to keep it contained. He turned back to Holly. "I know you're probably busy getting packed up, but I thought I'd at least stop in for a minute if that's okay."

"Oh. Sure. Right." She glanced behind her and then gestured for him to follow. "You can come in here if you want."

Pierce followed her down the hall. He glanced into the other doorway, which must have been Dahlia's room. The suitcase was open on the bed. Clothes had been packed inside, and others were waiting on the comforter to go in next. The drawers were open to showcase their emptiness.

He turned away and went into Holly's bedroom.

No, not *her* bedroom. Just the bedroom she was renting. Still, there was that intimate feeling of being in someone else's bedroom. Her dark green suitcase was visible through the open closet door, and her makeup and perfume had been neatly arranged on the dresser. Her laptop and file folders were scattered on the bed with a sprinkling of pens and highlighters on top.

"How's your dad doing?" She waved him into the chair in the corner while she perched on the bench at the end of the bed. "I feel so bad for him."

"Well enough. He's settling in with me until he gets things figured out." The logistics of fitting his father into his apartment weren't at the forefront of his mind, though Rick's words were. He only had so much time, and he couldn't waste it. There was something between them. Pierce knew it was important, and the time crunch was very real. His words hit a wall in his throat and refused to come out.

"That's kind of you." She pressed her lips together and looked away as she hugged her knees.

Why should it be so awkward to be there with her? Things definitely hadn't been when he'd brought her to Selene's and then back to his place. For those few hours, Pierce had felt like the two of them were truly mates, that they fit together as perfectly as puzzle pieces. Now, his wolf still knew the truth. That didn't make it any easier to get past the reality of the situation surrounding them. "You're leaving tomorrow, right?"

She ducked her head toward her knees and frowned. "Yeah."

"Are you all packed and ready?" It was small talk, nothing that meant anything, but as he said it, he became curious. She and Dahlia seemed to be in very different stages of getting ready to leave.

Holly shook her head, making her dark hair caress her shoulders. "Not yet, but I've been caught up with my writing. I didn't bring much anyway, so I'll just throw it all together in the morning."

"Do, um, do you and Dahlia need a ride to the airport?" It was a desperate attempt to spend more time with her, even though he'd only be teasing himself if she agreed.

"No," Holly said quickly. "We've got that taken care of, with the rental car drop-off and everything."

"Right. Sorry. I wasn't thinking." He knew how badly he wanted her. Not just physically—although he could certainly imagine what the two of them might do if they had this place all to themselves at the moment—but in every way. When she left, he'd be lonely. He'd sit at home or at the firehouse and wonder what might've happened if things had worked out differently, if he'd asked if there might be a way for things to work out. He'd lay in bed at night and think about the softness of her hair or the vibration of her laughter against his chest. He'd be miserable.

Something made him look at the suitcase again. She'd packed her life into it, just as she did every year. That didn't mean she could make a home there or that she even wanted to. She had a life back in Cape Cod. It wasn't up to him to make her change that.

Given the way she was acting, he was pretty sure she didn't want him to. Holly was barely looking at him, studying her toes or the floor instead of his face. She hadn't run into his arms to greet him, glad to see that he'd stopped by. Instead, she played the obliged hostess, bringing him into the house but not into her heart.

He stood. "I'm sorry. I know you're busy, and I should've called before I came over. I just wanted to thank you for a nice time and say goodbye."

"Thank you, and thank you for taking me out," she replied politely as they moved toward the front door.

It was a polite exchange, but there was nothing

more between them than two high school kids who'd gone out simply because their parents were good friends and thought they'd like each other. Pierce hesitated in the doorway, wondering if there was something else he could do. She'd told him all about how gorgeous Cape Cod was, how comfortable and happy her little home was, how she'd spent far too much time decorating her office space so that it would be perfect when she was writing away. There was no room for him in that life, nor could he rip her out of it and expect her to be a part of his.

"I was happy to," he replied honestly. Pierce leaned down and pressed his lips against hers, giving himself one last thing to cling to during the long nights ahead. "For what it's worth, I wish we could've figured out a way to spend more time together, to get to know each other. I know what we have between us is special, even if it can't last."

She twisted her fingers together, looking down at her feet and then back up at him. "Me, too. I know sometimes people try long-distance relationships, but that's *really* long."

The distance was one he was painfully aware of. Pierce had never been to Massachusetts, but already he could feel every mile like a stab in his heart. "I guess that's just as well. I come from an old-fashioned pack, and the differences between us might make things difficult."

Holly tipped her head back and narrowed her eyes. "They already don't like me?"

"I think it's quite the opposite." Pierce checked quickly to make sure Dahlia wasn't around. "It's just that we have a tradition of marking our mates. I know that's a rare thing these days, even among wolves."

She lifted her brows. "How would something like that work between a wolf and a bear?"

"I don't know," he admitted, and he supposed he'd never get a chance to find out. "No one's ever done it before that I'm aware of. Anyway, now I'm just making excuses for standing here longer. I'll go. If it matters, I'll miss you."

"Me, too."

He walked out the door and to his car. That was it. His mate was about to fly off home, and he would be alone. It was over as quickly as it'd begun.

9

"Where are we going next?" Holly tried to keep a light inflection in her voice, even though she wasn't feeling it. She'd been following Kyle all over Eugene for the last two days and had yet to figure out exactly what his process for this article would be. Her feet hurt, and she was starting to think she should've just gone home.

Of course, if she had, that meant she would've been leaving Pierce and everyone else like him vulnerable to Kyle. The guy could be an absolute pest, but he'd proven himself within Newman Media Group to be driven and determined. If he thought there were shifters out there, he was going to find them. Holly just had to hope the other shifters didn't find out about them first.

Kyle walked slowly through the Whiteaker neighborhood, his head swiveling and his eyes alight. "Anywhere and everywhere," he replied quietly.

"That seems a bit more random than I would've imagined," she mumbled.

He let out a superior laugh. "Holly, honey, you're an excellent writer. You know how to immerse someone in a whole new world. But it's *my* job to find that world in the first place so you can write about it. A subject like this is going to be the kind that hides in plain sight, one that's everywhere, yet no one talks about it. We need to talk to everyone from the humble grocery store clerk to the mayor."

That was going to take a hell of a long time. Not that Holly wanted to point him in the right direction and expose the shifter community, but if they got down to the nitty-gritty, she might be able to figure out a way to stop him and put this whole thing to bed. "You don't really think they're just mingling with regular society, do you? I mean, you mentioned you thought a lot of people at that club might be involved. What was it called? Selma's?"

"Selene's," he corrected. Kyle waited to continue until someone had passed them on the sidewalk. "And yes, I think it's a virtual hotbed. I also think it's a quick way to get caught. We have no idea what these people are really like, Holly. They probably look just like you and me on the outside, but I wouldn't trust them. For all I know, they eat people like us for breakfast."

Maybe people like you. Two days was too long to be playing dumb, especially to someone like Kyle. He had no idea she was only there to keep an eye on him and try to deter him from this article. So far, she felt like she was doing a good job of it. He thought she was really in on it, ready to share her byline with the great Kyle Freeman. The problem is that it meant she had to spend an awful lot of time with him. "Even if you find them, how will you get proof of who they are?"

"*What* they are," he corrected. "They're definitely not human."

She suppressed her bear and her anger at that response. "Anyway," she continued through gritted teeth, "how are you going to get proof? You can't just walk up to someone and ask them to, you know..."

"Change before my very eyes?" He turned to her, taking her by the arms. "Holly, all I have to do is find out who and where they are and then track down their routine. I'll worry about the proof afterwards. Video, probably."

"No one will believe that's real, considering how easy it is to manipulate video these days with AI," she pointed out. "Just think about all those viral clips that go around."

He let out an impatient sigh. "Fine. Then I'll just capture one. Whatever it takes, Holly."

A shiver of dread rippled through her, and her bear recoiled at Kyle's words. Capture? That was exactly what every shifter she knew feared the most. Humans had a tendency to trap anything they didn't understand, as long as they didn't kill it first. It wasn't likely that a singular journalist could actually achieve this, but the very idea of it filled her with apprehension.

"The locals know something," Kyle reasoned as he stopped and opened the door to a little place called First Light Café. "Eventually, we're going to talk to the right one."

"Good morning!" a woman behind the counter called. "Have a seat anywhere, and I'll come get your order in a minute."

It was a cozy place, and Holly was happy to sink into a padded chair. Plenty of indirect light came in through the front windows, giving the café a comfortable glow. She picked up the menu on the table and glanced it over, pleased and surprised that everything looked so healthy. "Oh, look. A loaded breakfast potato. That sounds so good."

"Uh-huh." Kyle had a menu as well, but he was furtively looking over the top of it at the other patrons. He looked like he belonged on some cheesy spy show and needed only a trench coat and a fedora to complete the scene.

"All right, folks. Sorry, that took me a minute. I was just finishing up a batch of pumpkin walnut muffins. What can I get for you?" The woman who'd greeted them took a pen from behind her ear and held it expectantly over her ordering pad, watching them with soft brown eyes.

"Well, Tiffany," Kyle said after he'd glanced at her nametag, "I think I'll take the avocado toast."

Tiffany sighed. "That normally comes on sprouted bread, as it says on the menu, but we keep getting shorted by our supplier. I do have twelve-grain or whole wheat."

"Twelve-grain is fine," he said hurriedly, not really caring about the food at all, "and an unsweetened tea."

"And for you, dear?" Tiffany turned to Holly.

She was a shifter. Holly could tell right away, but the longer Tiffany stood there at their table, Holly knew for sure. An animal lived inside her, but it wasn't dangerously lurking as Kyle imagined. "The loaded breakfast potato sounds good. And you mentioned the pumpkin muffins, so I think I'll have one of those, too."

"Is it all right if that comes out about five minutes after your potato? I've just about got them done."

A warm, fresh, homemade pumpkin muffin. Holly would wait hours for that. "Sure. And some coffee."

"Great choices. Can I get you guys anything else?"

Holly shook her head, but Kyle had other ideas. "Actually, yes, although nothing that's on the menu. I was wondering if there have been any strange occurrences in the area."

A strand of Tiffany's dark blonde hair had fallen loose from her bun, and she tucked it behind her ear. "Strange occurrences? I'm not sure what you mean."

"Oh, you know, anything a bit...different. The kind of news that traditional outlets wouldn't publish. We're reporters specializing in the paranormal," Kyle explained, raising his eyebrows and cocking his head as though that should enchant this woman into telling him everything he wanted to know.

"Paranormal investigators? You mean, like, ghost hunting?" Tiffany asked. "I don't think I know anything about that."

"No, not just ghosts." Kyle was trying to get her to come around and say it instead of throwing it out there himself. "Anything that's not about regular humans, if you know what I mean. The kind of stories all the locals know but no one else talks about."

"I think I do," Tiffany said with a smile. "We have tons of stories around here about Sasquatch."

Kyle shook his head. "No, not Bigfoot."

"He prefers to be called Sasquatch," Tiffany replied. "It's more respectful. He's got quite the following around here, and I even know someone who's quite an expert in the field."

Holly clenched her teeth, holding back a laugh.

"No," Kyle said, more forcefully now. "Not ridiculous things like that. I'm looking for *real* stories."

Holly caught the woman's eye. "Sorry," she mouthed, knowing that Kyle was taking up her time.

The corner of Tiffany's mouth ticked up slightly. "Oh, the Sasquatch is definitely real. I'm sure some of the sightings are just excited campers who hear a deer in the woods and want it to be something more, but I know people who've actually seen him. Right up close and personal."

She was playing with him! It was getting harder to hold herself together now, knowing that this woman was purposely derailing Kyle's line of questioning instead of just saying no.

"Never mind," Kyle finally grumbled.

"I'll have your food right out," Tiffany promised.

Once she finally felt like she could speak without laughing, Holly leaned forward. "Do you find that people actually just open up and tell you things? Strangers in a café just confessing their weird experiences?"

"Yes, actually." His voice was hard. Tiffany dropped off their drinks, and then he continued. "Usually, when something like this is going on, someone knows about it, and they're just waiting for the right person to come along and listen to them. If it's not this woman, it's someone else."

"Hopefully."

"Think about it, Holly," Kyle insisted. "If people are into Bigfoot around here—"

"Sasquatch," she corrected.

He glared at her. "Anyway, if they believe in *that,*

then what we're looking for can't be too much of a stretch."

"Maybe not." She'd have to continue to play along for now. Their encounter with Tiffany reminded her of just how closely most people of their kind guarded their secret. A few young guys from the club had messed up, but everyone else would make up for it. Kyle would never find proof. If she babysat him for just a little longer, she could return to her regular life.

Their food arrived, and it was just as delicious as Holly had imagined. The textures and flavors put her in absolute heaven. She quickly made mental notes about the experience, and of course, she'd be leaving Kyle out of the picture if she did end up writing about it.

As they returned to the car a while later, Holly looked around. She only knew a handful of people in Eugene, and they were the ones who worked at Newman headquarters. Then there was Pierce. What were the chances she might run into him? What would she say if she did?

"You know, maybe the Bigfoot thing isn't so far off," Kyle speculated as they got in his sedan.

"Hm?"

"What are the chances that people are seeing a

monster in the woods and then attributing it to a legendary creature that they're familiar with? A large man with fur all over his body doesn't sound so far off from a shifter, really. Hell, I saw those guys turn into wolves, but there's always a chance that these people can do some other sort of shapeshifting."

"Lions, tigers, and bears?" she asked, unable to resist.

He hit the brakes a little too hard at a stop sign. "I thought you were in on this."

She'd gone too far, and she'd have to fix that before he realized the very subject he wanted to study was right under his nose. "I am. I'm sorry. I just use humor when I get a little scared, and the idea of these things wandering around has gotten me a little worried." Maybe that was swiveling too far back in the other direction, but it played to his lack of sensibility perfectly.

His jaw and his eyes hardened. "Don't worry about that, Holly. I'm going to keep you safe. I'm going to keep all of humanity safe from these beasts."

He couldn't see her smirk as she turned to look out the window. She caught sight of a man walking into the bank and, for a moment, thought it was Pierce, but when he turned his head, she saw that it wasn't. He'd looked so sad when he'd come to say goodbye to her, and she'd felt so guilty. She still did because she hadn't been honest with him. He'd been sweet enough to see her one last time before she left town, but she hadn't left at all. Several times in those short few minutes they'd been together, she'd almost told him about Kyle's project. She'd even convinced herself that he might be able to help her. But Holly wanted to protect him and all the other shifters in the area from Kyle, and she couldn't do that if Pierce were right there with her.

No, she probably wouldn't see him again. She'd been able to extend her stay at the little Airbnb, and unless she set fire to it, Pierce was a thing of her past. It was for the best, she knew, but her bear roiled inside her every time they turned a corner. It longed for him.

Holly knew she'd just have to get used to that feeling, no matter how awful it was.

10

"I can't believe Jack is already looking at colleges," Hayden said wistfully, shaking his head. He sat on the couch at the firehouse, flipping through several brochures and booklets his son had given him. "Don't get me wrong. I'm not complaining, especially since it wasn't all that long ago that I didn't even know if he was going to live. I'm just overwhelmed by how much there is to think about now that he's getting toward the end of high school."

Pierce drummed his fingers on the arm of his chair. "He's a smart kid. He's going to do well."

"I'm hoping being on the track team will help him get some scholarship money. It'll only be a few years after he gets started that we'll be sending Paige off to college, too." Hayden set one booklet down and picked up another.

"She just turned fourteen," Pierce noted. "You've got time."

"It seems that way, but trust me. It really does fly when it comes to kids. She's in high school now, and her guidance counselor is asking what career path she's interested in."

"What does she have to say about that?" Pierce had to admire the way his brother treated his stepdaughter like his own. Paige still saw her father on a regular basis, so when her mother Jessica married Hayden, she just gained an extra parent and a couple of siblings. Their blended situation seemed to be working out well.

Though Pierce was happy for his brother, he couldn't help but dwell on his own situation. He got up and went to the fridge for a soda before moving to the window. He'd met the perfect woman. Holly was stunning and smart. He knew she was talented because it'd been easy to find some of her articles online. They had a spiritual and physical connection that left him feeling incredible. Now that it'd been pulled out from under him, Pierce felt like he was falling and would never stop. He'd just live the rest of his life waiting for the ground to come up and smack him.

"She put the class on her request form, so I hope she gets it. She might decide she's not interested in the medical field at all, but at least she'll have a chance to explore some opportunities. Pierce."

"Hm?"

"Did you hear what I said?"

"Sure. I was listening. Paige might want to go into something in the medical field."

"Okay, so you were. But I'm going to put you in the zoo if you want to keep pacing like a caged animal. Are you and Dad settling in okay?"

Pierce's already bruised heart sank a little lower as he glanced at the hallway where the fire chief's office was. He forced himself to sit back down. "Yeah, we're fine. My place isn't very big, but he doesn't take up much room. I moved a few things around to accommodate him, but then he just kept apologizing for it and made me wish I hadn't changed anything at all. He's worried about being a burden, even though he's the furthest thing from it."

"Well, Jessica and the girls will take him off your hands when they all go shopping tomorrow," Hayden promised. "They're looking forward to it."

"I think he is, too, but don't say it like that. It's really not a problem to have him there. Dad's done an awful lot for us over the years, so I'm glad I can help." Granted, it would've been much easier to help if his father just needed him to come pull the Christmas tree out of the attic or mow the lawn. Rick was just so damn sad, and Pierce didn't know how he could make that better.

Hayden shrugged. "He wouldn't want to inconvenience anyone, but it's probably a little more on his mind because of the timing."

Pierce had been picking at the tab on his soda, but he looked up. "What do you mean?"

"You know, with you and Holly. You hadn't seen anyone for a long time, and Dad moves in right as you're starting something new," his brother explained.

"I'm not starting anything new," Pierce replied bitterly.

"Sure, you are." Hayden reached over and playfully smacked his arm. "It's pretty obvious to anyone who has eyes. Don't be ashamed of it, especially if the two of you are having a good time while she's here. When is she supposed to go back to Massachusetts, anyway?"

"She already did," Pierce snapped. If things had

happened differently, he wouldn't have both his father and brother all over him about Holly. Then again, that meant he would've been going through all this alone. The three of them had always been a support system for each other.

"What?" Hayden put the college brochure back on the coffee table.

"Yeah. She was just here for a few days for her annual meeting, and then she went back home. She left a few days ago." Just as she'd planned and just as she'd do every year. Pierce had allowed himself a small spark of hope that he'd get to see her when she returned to Eugene, but a few days once a year wasn't enough to build a relationship on. His wolf was disturbed all over again, knowing his mate had been right there, then vanished like a ghost. It almost made it seem like it hadn't really happened, but he knew it had.

Hayden sat forward, resting his elbows on his knees, and looked at his brother closely. "But I just saw her yesterday."

"Not unless you transported yourself to New England," Pierce retorted, wishing he could do that himself. "It must've just been someone who looked like her."

"I'd agree with you if I only saw her when you

pulled her out of the water, but don't forget that you brought her around a second time. This was definitely her. She was at Stella's Slice with some guy."

Pierce's wolf instantly turned possessive, flailing inside him at this new tidbit of information. He calmed himself, knowing that Hayden was probably wrong. "What guy?"

"I don't know. I was just dropping off Ellie and Paige, so I wasn't in there long. He was kind of tall and slim, with short hair and a narrow face. Dark eyes and hair, but no one I knew. He was talking a lot, gesturing with his hands and getting all excited." Hayden shrugged again. "Maybe it was someone she worked with."

"Yeah, it probably was. A coworker of hers showed up the night I took her to Selene's. She introduced me to him." And Pierce had felt an instant dislike for him the moment he laid eyes on him. There was something disingenuous about the guy that got under his skin, but Pierce hadn't thought to ask Holly any more about him later. Even she seemed like she was only putting up with him because they worked for the same company, so why would she go out for pizza with him?

"What do you think this is all about?" Hayden asked slowly.

"I don't know," Pierce admitted. He only knew he didn't like it. "I went to her place to say goodbye the day before she left. She hadn't packed yet and said it was because she'd gotten caught up in her writing. She was going to do it the next morning instead."

Hayden pursed his lips. "I hate to say it, but it sounds like maybe she never packed at all."

"I don't understand why." Pierce ran his hands through his hair, feeling frustration build inside him. "There was something between us. She and I both knew it, and that was why she was so upfront with me about having to go back home. It doesn't make sense that she would throw that out there and then just not leave. Why wouldn't she tell me she was staying?"

"There must've been a miscommunication somewhere," Hayden replied, his voice soft and gentle.

Pierce gave his older brother a look. "Are you actually trying to do that same thing Dad does? Getting all subtle while indirectly telling me what to do?"

Hayden put his hands up. "Hey, all I can say is it works on the kids. You do what you want."

"That's easy for you to say now," Pierce grumbled. "I'm taking an extended lunch hour. I'll let you tell the chief, or maybe you can just drop an understated hint."

"I'll do that," Hayden promised.

Pierce got in his truck and headed across town. He wasn't actually mad at Hayden for trying to give him advice, and he couldn't blame either him or Rick for being light-handed with it. That was just how the three of them were. They didn't feel the need to boss each other around when being a little more laid back about things worked so well. No, the irritation in Pierce came from a completely different situation, one he hoped he could do something about.

Numerous thoughts raced across his mind, each dismissed as quickly as it came. Could Holly have lied to him because she wanted to date Kyle instead? No, there was no way. Pierce could tell Holly had the same dislike for Kyle that he did. Even if she had to put up with him, she wouldn't have stayed there for him.

Had Pierce done anything wrong to chase her away? If he had, it would've made more sense for her to just go back to Cape Cod and never speak to him again. It wouldn't explain her presence in Eugene.

She was a gifted writer. Perhaps her boss had

seen that and had asked her to stay longer for some important meeting. Holly wouldn't have told him because they'd already said their goodbyes, and dragging things out after that would only make it harder. That was at least as close as Pierce felt he could get on his own. With a little luck, he'd known the truth in a few minutes when he got to her place.

He just hoped she was still staying there. How far out of her way would she have gone to avoid him?

His wolf leaped up when he saw the same beige rental car sitting in the driveway as he came around the corner. So she was still there, and he'd have his chance to see what was happening. He'd already told himself several days ago that he wasn't going to try to make her stay, and she'd told him she had her own life to go back to. Pierce understood they could probably never work things out, so he wasn't there to change her mind. He was just there to find out why. He pulled in a deep breath and knocked on the door.

He waited, then knocked again. He looked for a doorbell, but there was none. Rubbing his teeth over his lips, he stepped back down into the driveway and laid his hand on the hood of her car. The metal was cold under his hand where the shadow of the house fell across it, so she likely hadn't driven anywhere that day, yet she wasn't there. Pierce went back up to the door and knocked again, just in case she'd been busy.

Why was she hiding from him, and why would she spend any time with that creep Kyle? What the hell was happening?

11

"Here we are." Kyle glided the car to a stop against the curb. He quickly turned off the headlights and made sure the dome light wouldn't kick on.

Holly spotted Selene's through the windshield. Kyle had parked on a side street across from it so they could see the front and side of the club. "I thought you said you didn't want to go back in there."

"I don't. We're just going to watch the place," Kyle explained. "We're going to document everyone going in and out of there. Some of them very well may be the same people who were there when we were, and they might even be the same guys I followed. They're the ones I'm really after, but I'll take whatever data I can get."

Holly's chest tightened as she spotted Max at the front door. She didn't doubt Pierce's other pack members, like Rex and Lori, were in there. He'd introduced her to several others throughout the night, though they were a blur since she'd been so focused on him. "But you don't know if any of these other people are shifters," she reasoned.

"They're still associating with them. I can't explain it, but I've got a feeling this place is a big hangout for them. I've got a buddy in the tech industry. I'm going to send all the information to him to see if he can run it through a recognition system or see if any of them have features in common. We have to figure out how we're going to spot these guys."

Damn. He was starting to sound like he actually had a plan, even if it was complete lunacy. "It doesn't seem right to just sit here and spy on people."

"There's a lot of that in my line of work," Kyle insisted. "Investigative reporting is all about patience and observation. Of course, it doesn't hurt to have a handsome face. It gets people to open up a little more easily."

Oh, great. He'd gone back to arrogance again. Holly didn't want to feed his ego since it was already stuffed full, but she had to be careful. She'd already made too many sarcastic or critical remarks, and it wasn't like she could stop this investigation by telling Kyle it was silly. She had to find a way to convince him, but for the moment, he had to believe she was on his side. "I'm sure that's true."

His eyes had been focused on the rock club, but he quickly turned to look at her with a smirk. "So you've finally noticed?"

"I mean, um—" She floundered for a good reply that wouldn't completely shoot him down nor encourage him too much. "You did get that one woman to open up earlier today. The one outside the pizza shop."

"Yes, she certainly had a good story to tell. I have a feeling her entire life will change once we get the truth out there."

Holly wasn't convinced. The woman had been sitting on the corner with a cardboard sign, begging for money and food. Holly had given her a bit of both without asking for anything in return, but Kyle had decided to interview her about strange activity in the neighborhood. He'd made the mistake of feeding her information about exactly what he'd wanted, and the woman had instantly agreed with him. "Oh, yes! I've seen them! I see them all the time! They're everywhere!"

"You know, your entire life is about to change, too," Kyle continued. "You've been right here with me for every step of this work so far, and I know your writing is going to really bring this thing to life once we have all the evidence." He leaned over the console, his eyes shining in the streetlight. "What do you say we share more than just a byline?"

Holly blinked. Kyle had always hit on her at previous meetings, and he'd never really seemed to take the hint that she wasn't interested. In fact, it wasn't until this whole idea of exposing shifters came about that he'd started behaving more like a normal person. Apparently, he'd just been biding his time. "What?"

He tipped his chin down, trying to give her a smoldering look. "Come on, Holly. We're both mature adults, and I think it's time we were honest with each other. We've been spending an awful lot of time together, and the tension between us just keeps building."

The only tension she'd been feeling was just how awkward it was to go around town with him while he interrogated random strangers. "Uh, I don't know about that."

"I admit that I brought us on this little stakeout because it would help our project, but there were some other motivations behind it." He reached out and put his hand on her knee.

She picked it up and set it back near the gear shifter. "Kyle…"

"Yes. Say my name, Holly. I like hearing it come from your lips like that. We both know we can only resist this attraction between us for so long." He put his hand back on her knee, sliding it up a little.

"Hey!" He'd always just been a creep from a short distance before, but he'd never gone so far as to touch her. She picked up his hand and once again put it back on the console. "I'm here with you because we're *working* together," she reminded him.

Kyle let out a scoffing laugh. "If you're concerned about workplace ethics, don't be. I've spoken at length with Lorelei in HR, and we don't have anything to worry about since we don't work in the same office."

"I bet you have," Holly retorted. "You're not listening to me, Kyle."

"That's because your body and your mouth always have two very different things to say, Holly. I think it's time we shut one of those up for good, don't you?" He leaned further toward her, bringing his lips in toward hers.

Holly's hand shot out, grabbing his throat as she shoved him back onto his side of the car. "I never wanted anything to do with you, Kyle, and I never will. For someone who prides himself so much on discovering the truth, you sure don't know how to get the hint!"

Kyle floundered against the car window, gagging and choking from the force of her rebuttal. "You didn't have to do that!" he gasped.

"Obviously, I did." Holly's bear had made her, but she didn't regret it for a second. "I've tried being nice, and I've tried being direct. If you think we've been spending all this time together for any reason other than the story, you're a complete imbecile."

"Fine." He rubbed his throat, scrunching his face at the pain. "I get it, okay? We'll just focus on the story from now on."

That was exactly why she'd stayed in Eugene in the first place, but she knew she couldn't be in close proximity to this man any longer. "Hell, no. I've wasted far too much time on you and your story already, especially since there *is* no story!"

He had the nerve to look offended. "Are you saying you don't believe me?"

"Are you fucking kidding me? *No one* will believe you!" She knew the truth, the very truth that he was after, but that didn't matter anymore. "Despite what you think you've seen, and whatever proof you think you've got, this story won't be accepted anywhere. You sound like a raving lunatic, following random people around and insisting that they can turn into animals. No decent media source or even any other journalist will support you in this, and I refuse to have my name associated with yours in any capacity!"

His jaw dropped. Kyle gaped at her for a long moment, his eyes ping-ponging back and forth as he studied her face. He slowly started to nod. "I think I see what's going on here. It's that Pierce guy."

Panic and rage moved through her body, boiling under her skin. She couldn't let him think he was onto something, not when the shifters Kyle had seen could very well have been some of Pierce's packmates. Her bear was furious at the idea of Kyle saying anything against her mate. Guilt immediately swallowed her, knowing that she'd lied to him. "The more you talk, the less sense you make."

"No, I understand now. That Pierce guy must be one of them. That's why he brought you to Selene's. He knows the place because that's where they all hang out. He's got you brainwashed, or maybe even worse. Holly, there's no telling what he's going to do to you. Come on, I'm going to get you out of here."

"The fuck you are!" Holly snagged her bag and shoved open her car door before Kyle could get the ignition going. "Go home, Kyle. There's nothing here for you." She slammed the door and charged down the sidewalk.

His headlights followed her. True fear rose inside her now, wondering if and when he'd become suspicious of her as well. That bouncer Max was probably just across the street in the shadow of the doorway of Selene's. He would probably help her, but getting him involved would put him at risk. She couldn't do it. She was alone.

Finally, at the intersection, Kyle turned off. She breathed a sigh of relief and opened the rideshare app on her phone.

"Hey, are you okay?" the young man behind the wheel asked when she opened the backdoor.

Holly sensed the animal inside him and relaxed her shoulders a little. His identity didn't make him safe, but it still made her feel better. "Yeah. I'm just having a bad night."

"There are snacks in the seat pocket and a cooler

of bottled waters back there if you need anything. Help yourself."

"Thank you." Holly hesitated, but when she reached into the seat pocket and found a little bag of dried cherries covered in chocolate, she tore straight into them. They wouldn't make the whole world better, but they helped. She was going to leave a generous tip for this guy.

"Um, ma'am?" he said when he pulled up. "I just want you to know there's a man on the porch."

"What?" Her heart skipped a beat, then skipped another when she looked. "I know him, but thanks for the heads up."

Yeah, he was definitely getting a good tip. It was easy to just get a ride back to her rented house, but now she had to figure out how to deal with the problem that was waiting for her. "Pierce? What are you doing here?"

"I came to ask you the same thing," he replied. His voice was gruff but not harsh as he stood and came down the stairs. "I thought you left."

"I planned to." How could she explain it all to him now? "I had something come up."

"Work?"

She couldn't quite see his face with the porch light behind him, but she heard the hurt and the hope in his voice. "Sort of. Come inside and I'll tell you."

He followed her in and she shut the door. Holly locked the deadbolt, then peeked through the front curtain, just in case. When that driver had told her a man was on her porch, she'd thought for sure Kyle had gotten to her place first. The relief she'd felt at knowing it wasn't him was short-lived. She could've found a way to deal with Kyle. This was harder.

"Is someone following you?" Pierce asked.

"Probably not." The chocolate-covered cherries had whetted her appetite, and she went to the fridge. There wasn't much food there, and she hadn't had much cause to cook since Kyle had insisted on going to so many restaurants during their investigation. She found a container of lunch meat and another of sliced cheese and put them out on the counter. Her bear rumbled with satisfaction, wanting all the proteins and fats. "Are you hungry?"

"No." He slid onto the stool at the breakfast bar, facing her as she dug into her snack.

He was waiting for an explanation, and she had to give it to him. He deserved that much. She should've told him in the first place. It was too late for that now, and all she could do was move forward.

"Do you remember that guy Kyle I introduced you to?"

The tendons in his neck visibly tightened. "Yes."

Jealousy looked good on him, something she couldn't help but notice even when she was emotionally exhausted and a bit embarrassed. "He's an investigative reporter. He specializes in digging up dirt that others are trying hard to hide. From my experience as a writer, I know I can't just turn off the process, and neither can he. He caught snippets of conversation that night at Selene's, which made him suspicious. He decided to follow some guys as they left, and he saw." Holly plucked another slice of cheese from the bag, knowing she didn't have to tell him exactly what Kyle had seen.

He swiped a hand over his forehead. "What happened?"

"Nothing in that moment. I think it scared the shit out of him and he ran away, but then he decided he was going to find the truth behind it. He wants to dig into this and expose all shifters. He's envisioning a nationwide headline with his name beneath it. And mine." She swallowed a bit of nausea that rode up with her words.

Pierce stared at her in disbelief. "You're doing this?"

"No." How could he think that? Then again, she'd already lied to him. What evidence did he even have that she was a decent person? "When he asked me to work with him, I knew I had to say yes. It was the only way to know for certain what he was up to and how close he was getting to the truth. Although I hate to admit it, I know he's good at his job, and I couldn't risk leaving him to it. So I stayed, and I've basically been following along with him to keep track of what he's doing."

"You could've told me," he replied thickly. "You've been in town, hanging out with him, and all this time, I thought you were gone."

Holly knew she didn't have to justify who she did or didn't spend time with. She understood why he was upset, but he had to understand this from her side, too. "That was part of the risk. I was trying to keep everyone who shared this identity as far away from him as possible."

"What about you?" Pierce challenged.

"I guess he had too much hubris to think he'd actually associate with one of us. I don't have a good answer for that, but I know I'm right about everything else." She relayed how Kyle had theorized about Pierce's role in this whole scheme. "I think it was only because I finally made him realize I'm not interested in him. His ego was hurt, and he wanted someone else to blame besides himself."

Pierce's knuckles turned white where they gripped the countertop. "So he made a pass at you?"

"He's been doing it for years, but I put him in his place." She was confident in that. Kyle might have plenty of crazy things coming out of his mouth, but she'd bet her life savings he'd never hit on her again after she'd slammed him in the throat. "Anyway, that's not really the point. The real problem at hand is that Kyle isn't going to stop until he knows the truth. I thought he'd get bored and move on to something else, but he's completely obsessed. He's absolutely convinced there are shifters, and he knows they congregate at Selene's. I don't know how I can stop him now, but I've got to figure something out."

Pierce's lips twitched as he ran his tongue over his teeth. He straightened, staring at the kitchen wall. "I'll take care of it."

"What? No. Pierce, you can't do that. Like I said a minute ago, he already thinks you're a part of this. If you get involved, it'll only confirm that for him." Alarm bells clanged in her mind at the thought of

Pierce putting himself directly in the line of fire, so to speak.

"I won't do it alone. You didn't have to either, Holly. You know as well as I do that we have to rely on our connections to each other to keep guys like Kyle from taking us down. I'll contact my pack, and we'll come up with something. Rex is good at this sort of thing, and that's exactly why he's Alpha."

She opened her mouth, wanting to protest, but closed it again. He was absolutely right. If she'd been back home and had this sort of a problem, she would've gone to her Alpha, her cousin Dylan, and the rest of the Brigham clan. It was what she should've done in the first place, but at the time, it'd made more sense to ensure some distance between Kyle and his mark. "What can I do?"

"Just tell me what you know about Kyle's plans." He'd released his death grip from the counter and let out a deep breath.

Fate was cruel. It'd tied the two of them together, bonding them with a connection no one could break. Shifters waited for the right one to come along, and at forty-three, she'd certainly waited her fair share of time. In fact, she'd started to think she might never meet him. There he was, standing right in front of her, but the awkwardness and tension between them were so wrong. It shouldn't feel this way. Holly recounted everything she knew about Kyle's plans. "It seemed like he was really focused on Selene's, and he'd also mentioned going back to Skinner Butte Park. That was where he saw the wolves before."

"All right. I'll take care of this." Pierce turned toward the door.

"Pierce." She followed him, not wanting him to go, yet knowing he should. "For what it's worth, I'm really sorry this worked out the way it did."

He hesitated with his hand on the knob. "Yeah, me too. Is there anything else I need to know?"

It felt like a jab, an unfair question that reminded her of her lie, but she couldn't blame him. The trouble was, Holly thought there just might be something else she needed to say. She had to be completely sure before she did, though. "No. I don't think so."

"I'll let you know what happens." He opened the door and then looked back over his shoulder. "Lock this behind me."

"I will." She pushed the door in place and then flicked the deadbolt over with a heavy thunk, feeling like she was locking her mate out of her life instead of just protecting herself.

She'd wanted to keep him safe, and she hadn't been able to. This whole trip had been terrible, and Holly knew things would never be the same again.

12

Rex slowly rubbed his jaw as he listened to the last of Pierce's words. "Interesting."

Brody nodded. "Every now and then, we get some crazy human who insists they want to expose us. I just looked this guy up, though. He's not just a random guy with a cell phone camera. He's a legitimate journalist, and he seems to be a fairly well-respected one, too."

"I don't think he will be for long at the rate he's going," Pierce replied. Holly had recounted all the things Kyle had said, noting how wild and obsessive he sounded. If he were honest, the part that bothered him the most was how obsessive Kyle was about *her*. At least he could console himself, knowing that the feeling wasn't mutual, but it only helped so much when he knew how bad things were between Holly and him. He'd been angry with her for not telling him the truth in the first place. It should've brought them closer once she explained it all, but it felt like it only pulled them further apart.

"Maybe not, but we still have to stop this before it goes any further," Max said. He looked at the photo of Kyle that Brody had pulled up on his phone. "I remember him. I didn't have a good reason not to let him into Selene's, even though I had a bad feeling about him. I should've followed my instincts."

"Don't blame yourself for any of this. I don't make it a policy to keep humans out of my club," Rex reminded him. "If you want to point the finger at anyone, it needs to be whoever was careless enough to shift where they could be seen."

"Any idea who that was?" Brody asked.

Pierce shook his head. "Not a clue, other than that they were pretty young."

"That could be anyone," Rex said.

Jimmy, who'd come out of the garage long enough to see what the issue was, tapped his fingers on the table. "It's not the first time something like this has happened. The problem usually takes care of itself. No one will believe a man who swears he saw a guy turn into a wolf. It sounds ludicrous to anyone who doesn't know the truth."

"I think that's what Holly was gambling on," Pierce told the retired Alpha. "It doesn't seem to be working with this guy. He hasn't even been able to find any good proof, but that seems to only drive him further."

Jimmy let out a dry laugh. "Well, then, maybe we should give him all the proof he wants."

Rex nodded, a smile creeping across his face. "You just might be right, Dad. If this Kyle is determined to find shifters, then we let him find us on our own terms."

"He followed some young, overly confident guys out of the club and to the park," Pierce added, catching on to what they meant. "If he's focusing in on Selene's again, it wouldn't be difficult to set him up for another encounter."

"I want to do it." Hunter had been listening quietly at his father Max's side, but now he sat forward and even raised his hand a little.

"You sure?" Max asked. "Not that I don't think you could handle him, but it definitely means putting yourself at risk."

Hunter nodded. "Yeah. Absolutely. I could even bring Conner with me. We'll go to the club, we'll drop a few hints, and then we'll walk out. It'll be like recreating what the guy has already seen, so we know he'll fall for it."

"The rest of us can be waiting in the park, so you'll have plenty of backup when you get there," Brody suggested.

"And we'll post a few guards along the way, just in case things get out of hand," Rex added. "I think Kane is on police duty tonight, so maybe he can make that area part of his patrol. Maybe Sean and Caleb will be available."

Hunter made a sour face. "Connor and I don't need that much help."

"It's not that I don't think you guys can do it," Rex assured him. "It's a simple matter of making sure everyone is safe."

Jimmy nodded. "That's something you'll always have to keep in mind when you become Alpha one day."

"That and the fact your mothers will kill me if I don't do everything to make sure you don't get a scratch on you," Rex added.

Jimmy laughed. "That's the other important part of being an Alpha. Keep the women happy!"

As Rex made a few phone calls to get things started, Pierce leaned back in his chair and wished he knew a way to keep his woman happy. It was impossible, though. They would get this Kyle issue taken care of, and then she really would leave town. There was no winning.

An hour later, he stood in the trees of Skinner Butte Park next to Hayden.

"You hanging in there?" his brother asked.

Pierce knew there was much more to that question than just casual conversation. He leaned against the bark of a Douglas fir, feeling it dig into his shoulder. "Not exactly."

Hayden leaned against the other side of the tree. "When I heard about all this, I wasn't sure if it meant you and Holly had figured things out or...the opposite."

"Nothing has changed," Pierce told him. "We've got this situation to deal with, but it doesn't make things any different for the two of us."

"Let me ask you something." Hayden leaned forward. "Do you want to be with her?"

How could he not? She'd technically lied to him, but no matter how bitter Pierce felt about it, he knew she was just doing her best. It made his wolf rage with jealousy to know how much time she'd been spending with Kyle, especially in close quarters, but she'd only done it to try to keep everyone else from getting hurt. "Of course I do."

"Then you need to figure out a way to make it happen," Hayden replied. "If you don't want the Dad routine, I'll just give it to you straight. Work it out, whatever it takes, or you might regret it later."

Movement in the shadows caught Pierce's eye. Two forms took shape on the path that ran through the woods, right where some of the park lights still shone on them. "They're here."

The park around them went silent as Hunter and Connor reached the tree line. Limned in light, they stopped. They were just a couple of young guys who'd been out at a rock club. Max had served his normal function at the door of Selene's. He'd confirmed that Kyle had been bold enough to come back inside, despite his fear of being caught, and that he'd followed Hunter and Connor back out. Kane had spotted them along the way. He'd also spotted Kyle, who'd gone back to his car and drove it to the edge of the park instead of following the young men directly.

Looking at them now, Pierce wondered if he would've had the balls to do something like this at their age. Hunter and Connor glanced around, careful not to look directly behind them, then let their humans go. They made a quick shift into their wolves, dropping to all fours and shaking out their tails before moving slowly down the path.

Pierce's heart hammered inside his chest as Kyle appeared on the path behind the boys. He kept his distance, moving slowly and carefully for a human, but no wolf ever would've missed the noise of his footsteps behind them. Hunter and Connor had carried out their part of the plan. Now, it was time for Pierce to carry out the part he'd volunteered for. He stepped away from the tree and out onto the path. "Kyle. Nice to see you."

The journalist came to a quick halt. Fear crossed his face for a moment before he managed to get it under control. He looked in the direction Hunter and Connor had gone and then back at him. "Hey. Pierce, is it?"

He knew damn well what his name was. "So you do remember me. I'm surprised to see you here. I thought everyone who came in for the Newman meeting had gone back home. What keeps you in Eugene?"

Kyle lifted his chin. "I think you know exactly what it is. You're one of them, aren't you?"

Pierce knew he had plenty of backup, but he

didn't need it. He almost wished he was alone with Kyle. His wolf reminded him what he could do if he really wanted to, but he restrained it. For the moment. "One of what?" he challenged softly.

"A wolf," Kyle spat. "You're a goddamn wolf!"

"Really?" Pierce stretched out his arm and straightened his fingers, examining his skin. "I look like a regular human to me."

But Kyle wouldn't back down. "I saw them, and I know they exist. You're protecting them, and you were only getting close to Holly to make sure she didn't find out. You were using her!"

Pierce snagged Kyle's collar, twisting the material in his fingers as he yanked him close. He could feel control slipping away, and he wanted so badly to let it go entirely. "We can talk about who's using Holly, but it sure as shit isn't me. You only want her in on your little story to make your sorry ass look better."

"So she told you?" Kyle pushed uselessly at Pierce's hand. "That only proves my point! You charmed her so she wouldn't expose your secret!"

"You've got it all twisted up inside that narrow head of yours." Pierce felt his fangs pressing at the insides of his gums, threatening to descend at any moment. He could tear this guy apart with little effort, regardless of what form he was in. He wasn't worth it, though. He let go of Kyle with a shove.

The journalist stumbled backward and fell on his ass. "I know what I saw. I know what's going on here, and I'm going to prove it!"

Pierce spread his hands. "If you want wolves, I'll give you wolves." Behind him, the others stepped out of the trees. Rex, Brody, and Hayden emerged on two feet and quickly shifted to four. Hunter and Connor stepped out and joined them, still in their animal forms.

Pierce took pleasure in seeing the sheer terror on Kyle's face as his fellow pack members stepped up to make a semicircle behind him. "I'm going to give you one chance, Kyle. Drop the story. Forget what you think you saw and forget what you're seeing here right now. Let it all go and pretend it never happened, and you'll never see another shifter again."

Kyle's heels dug into the grass as he shoved himself backward. He gulped and gasped as he watched the encroaching pack of wolves, his eyes wild with fear. "How do I know you won't just kill me anyway?"

"I'm a man of my word," Pierce replied. "If I

make a promise, I follow through with it. If I let you look into the situation a little more, I think you'd find we're all that way. Every single one of us."

Staggering to his feet, Kyle backed away some more.

"We're not interested in hurting you or anyone else," Pierce continued. "We just want to live our lives in peace. I don't think that's too much to ask, do you?"

"How many of you are there?" Kyle asked, his eyes darting back and forth.

How could Pierce answer that safely? He'd been trained from childhood to pretend their kind didn't exist at all, yet he needed Kyle to know it wasn't just this small group that would want revenge if he carried out his plan. "Thousands. We're all over the place. You can't avoid us, and we won't let you do this to us."

Kyle swallowed as he took several more steps back. "I…I…"

Pierce took a singular step toward him. "Kill the story."

"Never! They deserve to know the truth!" Kyle turned and ran.

His beast had been fighting to break free all day. As Pierce bolted forward, his wolf sprang out of him.

Fur exploded on his skin as his back lengthened and his tail swished through the air. His paw pads landed on the grass beneath him as he and the others chased Kyle through the park. Saliva dripped from his jaws, and once again, Pierce was reminded of just how easily they could take Kyle down permanently.

Easy, Rex's voice echoed in his head, making Pierce realize he'd been thinking about it harder than he'd realized. *We can't go that far with this.*

He was right, but what else were they going to do?

Kyle moved faster than Pierce had imagined. He sprinted to his car and jumped inside, firing up the engine. Pierce reached the back of the vehicle as the brake lights went off, slamming his paws into it. His claws carved deep marks through the paint, making the metal underneath shine in the park lights as the sedan screeched out of the parking lot.

What do you think? Brody asked as he trotted up beside Rex and Pierce. *Despite what he said, did we scare him enough to make him quit?*

Pierce wished that was the case, but he was starting to get a good idea of just how adamant Kyle was about this. *No. I think he's more dangerous than ever now.*

As the other Glenwood wolves began discussing

their next step, a sphere of concern began taking up space in Pierce's chest. They had to stop Kyle, yes. That was obviously important, but the man didn't have anything ready to take to the public. He could shout from the rooftops about the wolves who'd threatened him in the park, but he didn't have any real proof to back him up.

His more immediate concern was Holly. *I've got to go.*

Hayden angled up next to him, standing so that Pierce would have to go around him before he could leave. *Where?*

Holly's.

Rex turned to him. *Do you think she's in danger?*

His instincts were practically screaming at him. The way Holly had talked, she hadn't found any reason to be scared of Kyle. She felt she'd been able to put him in his place when he'd gone too far. But now he was a man with nothing left to lose, who felt with all certainty that the shifters were his enemies. *She's probably the person he knows best in town and the only one he's told about shifters. He thinks she's in danger from* us, *and I don't know what he's capable of.*

Then let's go, Rex urged.

They charged to the edge of the park before returning to their human forms so they could navigate through town by car. Though it would take too long and be too risky to try to get there in wolf form, it felt frustratingly slow to get around this way.

His wolf worried for her as they passed Selene's. She was trying to protect his secret, but had she protected her own well enough?

13

Holly balled up a shirt and slammed it into her suitcase. She couldn't just sit at her Airbnb and wait for Pierce to tell her he'd taken care of the Kyle situation. If she were honest with herself, she worried about how he and his pack planned to handle it in the first place. They wouldn't do anything too extreme, would they? Not that Kyle was her favorite person, and he'd certainly be risking the life of every shifter in the world by outing them, but she still didn't want anything bad to happen to him in return.

She yanked another shirt out of the closet, sending the hanger flinging upward in its wake. This whole thing was so frustrating! She'd thought she'd finally had a decent annual meeting—outside of almost drowning, of course. She'd met a fantastic guy who spoke to her very soul and seemed to be the embodiment of a modern-day hero. He was handsome, courteous, and everything else she'd want in a man.

"But then I had to go and fuck it up, didn't I?" she berated herself as she tossed the next garment into her suitcase, paying little attention to folding or organizing. It was just going to get shaken around in the belly of the plane, anyway. "I lied to him. I lied right to his face when I said I'd be packing up the next morning and leaving. I knew it was wrong, and it made me sick to do it. It was only because I wanted to protect him, but that obviously didn't work."

No, it sure hadn't. Now, he was out there taking care of the problem, putting himself right in the line of danger she'd tried so hard to keep him from. He had family there. He had backup and resources. Who was she to think she could stop this just because she knew Kyle and understood the process of creating an article?

"Hmph. Fucking Kyle." The jacket Holly had brought in case the nights were cool hit the open top of the suitcase and threatened to topple it backward. She'd only made herself look worse by spending her secret time in Eugene with her coworker. Again, she'd screwed things up beyond repair. Was she attempting to sabotage herself?

When she reached back into the closet, she grabbed the navy skirt she'd worn on her night out with Pierce. Tears welled up in her eyes as she ran her hands over the fabric, soft and flowy. It'd made her feel so sexy as it moved around her, but it was Pierce who'd truly made her come alive. She'd never felt so wanted as she had in his arms, and she'd never get to experience that again.

Holly brought the skirt over to her suitcase and laid it in gently. It was just a piece of clothing. It made no real difference in her life, but she knew it would always make her think of that night. It was a fateful night, with Rick's house burning down and all.

She pressed her lips together, wondering if it was even more fateful than that. Was there more to tell Pierce? She still had to figure that out.

Her phone chirped. It was too late for anyone to be calling or texting. Holly picked it up off the nightstand and saw the symbol for low battery. "I guess I really let myself get distracted today." She reached down for the charger, but it wasn't there.

After she checked the kitchen counter and the end table in the living room, Holly realized she must've left it in her car. Grabbing her keys, she stepped out into the night. She crossed the small patch of yard, realizing the grass was far brighter than it should be at this time. Turning, she looked up at the moon, full and bright as it shone down on her. Pierce had told her about the moon goddess Selene, whom Rex had named his club after. It was a new concept to her but one she'd grown to appreciate. The moon was always there, looking over them. Who was looking over her?

The screeching of tires had her turning again, this time toward the street as a car careened down it. The headlights bobbed and the brakes squealed as the vehicle curled into the driveway and nearly hit her rental.

"Hey!" she shouted, knowing what she'd have to pay for damages.

Kyle jumped out of the driver's seat. "Get in the house, Holly! Get inside right now and lock the doors!"

This guy just didn't give up. "What are you doing here?"

"Just get in the house. We can't talk out here." He grabbed her by the elbow and practically dragged her.

Holly went, but only because she knew Kyle.

He'd get whatever this was out of his system, and then she could get him to shut up and leave her alone for a while. She closed the door behind her but didn't lock it. "What do you want?"

"It's the shifters," he began. His hair was a mess, and his eyes were wide with dark hollows beneath them. The back of his jeans were muddy, and his shoes were dragging dirt and muck in that the landlord probably wouldn't be too happy about.

Holly put her hands on her hips. Kyle was a long way off from the neatly dressed reporter she knew from those annual meetings. Sure, he'd always been a creep, but he'd never looked like he'd been living under a bush before. "I thought I made it abundantly clear that I didn't want to discuss that anymore. I told you, there's no such thing."

"Oh, yes, there is!" He let out a maniacal laugh, a little too high in pitch. "I saw them with my own eyes, Holly. Not just one or two, and not just from a distance. A whole *bunch* of them."

Uh oh. "Were you drinking tonight?"

As seemed to be his habit, Kyle ignored anything that didn't play into his narrative. "Do want to hear the most interesting part? One of them was your little boy-toy, Pierce! He stood right there in front of me. He knew all about what I've been trying to do, and that only proves me right. He used you to get to me!"

That was absolutely not what happened, but she couldn't imagine how hysterical Kyle would get if she tried to explain fated mates to him.

"It wasn't just that," Kyle went on, pacing in front of her. "This wasn't just a man-to-man talk, Holly. He had his whole pack of wolves behind him, hackles raised and teeth bared. He threatened me and told me to stop. I refused and saw him turn, Holly, with my very own eyes—into a wolf! There are even scratches down the back of my car to prove it!"

Her stomach and heart sank. Pierce had tried, but Kyle was too stubborn to listen to any kind of reason. Even a snarling pack of wolves wasn't enough to drive him away from this story.

"You have to believe me, Holly," he insisted. "You have to, for your own safety! If they're coming after me, they're going to come after you, too!"

There wouldn't be any arguing with him. "Okay, Kyle," she said softly, speaking to him like a wild animal caught in a trap. "I believe you."

A small amount of relief showed in his eyes, but the frenzy he'd worked himself into wouldn't disappear with just an affirmation from her. "Good. Good.

I'm glad you're back on board, Holly. I need you in order to make this story work."

That was the very last thing *she* needed, as was him standing there in her temporary living room. She checked her back pocket for her phone, thinking she should probably at least send Pierce a text, but she'd left the damn thing in the bedroom. "So what's the next step?" she asked cautiously. If she could at least get information from him, she might be able to use it against him.

"I've been thinking about that a lot," he admitted, continuing to pace as he gestured wildly with his hands. "I worked with some ghost hunters last year on a story. They didn't find any evidence, of course, but they have some very sensitive equipment. Maybe they'd have some ideas as to how we could get infallible proof. Or they might even be able to tell the difference between humans and these monsters!"

She felt a familiar rise of anger within her. That was happening more and more around Kyle, especially when he was badmouthing a group of people he didn't even understand. She balled her hands into fists as her bear roared its discontent inside.

"I've got a buddy with high-res drone camera," Kyle continued. "I'd have to bring him out here from

Florida, but I wonder if he could fly over some of the parks at night and catch them in the act!"

"Even if they're real, don't you think it makes sense to treat them like any other people?" she asked. Holly knew Kyle was well past the point of being reasoned with, but she still had to try. She couldn't just give up on this.

"Ha!" he barked sharply. "They didn't treat *me* with any respect when they cornered me in the woods and threatened me, so there's no chance in hell that I'm going to give them the benefit of the doubt. You're too nice, honey. That's your problem."

"I know it is," she grumbled through gritted teeth as her bear surged once again, "but don't call me honey."

"I know for sure now that Selene's is a main hub for them. I followed a couple of guys out of there again tonight. Plus, at least two of the guys who work there were with Pierce tonight. I did a little bit of online research, wondering if anyone else had noticed strange activity there. I didn't find what I was looking for, but I *did* find that Selene was an ancient moon goddess. Think about it, Holly! The moon? People who change into wolves? It all makes sense!" He stabbed a finger toward his temple.

How was she going to fix this now? It'd gone too

far, too fast. Just a couple of days ago, he'd been raving at the woman in First Light Café, and Holly had been convinced he'd never go any further. Now, he was actually piecing a few bits of information together. The rock club being named after an ancient goddess meant nothing on its own, but he'd seen enough from Pierce and his packmates to understand there really was more here. They weren't werewolves, exactly, but his mind had defaulted to that because it could understand. "Kyle, I think we need to slow down and—"

"We're going to be so famous!" he rambled on, throwing his hands in the air. "Can you just imagine? This is going to be so much bigger than anything Newman publishes. You'll probably get job offers from all the biggest newspapers and magazines in the country. I might go into television."

He was definitely off the rails. "That's cool, but we really need to think about this."

"Or maybe they'll want us together, a package deal. Have you ever thought about television?"

Her anger continued to simmer inside her, working its way toward a rolling boil. She'd been putting up with him for the last several days. He'd probably cost her the last chance she had at a relationship with Pierce, if there had been one at all.

Now, he was determined to drag her along onto his rollercoaster ride of insanity. "No, and I'm not interested. I don't want to do any of this."

"Granted, nothing is going to top this story," Kyle continued. "This is the top, and once we milk this story for all it's worth, it'll be a bit of a downhill turn, but that's fine. I can handle that."

"Kyle, please."

"We just have to find a way to trap them, and I think you're the key. They don't think you're dangerous. No one does. Sweet little Holly, so shy and innocent. You're perfect!" He grabbed her by the arms, shaking her in his excitement.

"You're wrong," she growled, finally reaching a point of no return with all the emotions that bubbled inside her. Kyle refused to listen. It didn't matter if she pandered to him, tried to reason with him, or even grabbed him by the throat again. He was too damn stubborn. "I *am* dangerous, *honey*."

Holly stepped back and let her bear emerge. It'd been trapped inside her for too long, fighting against everything happening around her. She felt the familiar comfort of her dense fur. Her bones thickened and lengthened to support her massive muscles, and the deadly claws on the ends of her paws snagged in the carpet. Cracking sounds echoed through her skull as her bones rearranged into the other face she wore, the one with a long muzzle and dark nose. The lamp fell to the floor and crashed, the bulb sending up a pop of sparks as her large body tried to find enough room in the space.

A new sensation echoed deep inside her belly, a knowledge that she wasn't alone in this body. It was the confirmation she'd been seeking, and it filled her with a pleasant warmth. She was pregnant.

But Kyle was too busy shrieking for her to enjoy the moment.

With every ounce of exasperation she'd felt for Kyle, Holly pulled in a deep breath and let it out as a roar, screaming out her anger.

He fell backward over the coffee table and landed on his shoulder near the hearth, still bellowing. Kyle regained his footing, but there was no place to go unless he went past Holly. He threw his arms in the air, flailing about as he tried to figure out what to do about this black bear standing in his way.

Holly blinked. Her sight had always been good, and it was even sharper when she was in her animal form, but something didn't look right. The roots of his dark hair lightened as he gibbered before her, the effect moving out to the ends. His hair had turned a shocking shade of white.

Tired of all his bullshit and screaming, Holly raised her paw and sent it across his face with a smack. Kyle's eyes rolled back in his head, and he crumpled to the floor just as the front door flew open.

Holly backed away quickly. Instinctively, she wondered what sort of trap Kyle had set for her. But when she turned to the door to face the new danger, she saw it was only Pierce.

14

"She must've really knocked him good," Dawn said as she opened Kyle's eyes and checked them with a penlight as he lay on a couch in the Glenwood packhouse. "He's out, but there's no actual trauma to his head, no bruising. I think the only danger he's in right now is whatever danger he's brought upon himself." She turned off the light and straightened up.

Kyle wouldn't harm anyone in his current condition, but Pierce's wolf had yet to calm down since finding him at Holly's place. He rubbed his hand over the back of his neck. "What do we do with him?"

Rex came around to stand at his sister's side. "I can't help but think of the night I met Lori."

It seemed like an odd time to reminisce about such a thing, but Dawn nodded. "I was just thinking that, myself. It's not really all that different of a situation, is it?"

"Aunt Dawn? Can I do it?" Ava, Max's teen daughter, stepped hesitantly forward.

Dawn lifted an eyebrow. "You know how important this is, right? I'm not saying that to intimidate you, just to remind you of the stakes."

"I know, but I really think I can do it," Ava said, swallowing a little. Since discovering the abilities she'd inherited from the wolf-witch bloodline of the Glenwood females, she'd been eager to practice and develop her newfound skills whenever she could.

"Yeah, so do I, kiddo. Come on over here, and we'll mix the tincture." She brought Ava over to a table at the side of the room, where they began working with tiny glass vials of various liquids.

"I can't say I understand how it all works," Rex admitted to Pierce, "but we won't have anything to worry about from this guy once we're done with him. They'll wipe his memory of the whole thing, and he won't have any idea that he's ever seen a shifter."

"Good." Pierce looked down at Kyle, his jaw slack and his eyelids still. His chest rose and fell regularly, and he looked like he'd merely fallen into a deep sleep on the couch. His bright white hair made him look much older than he had earlier that night. "Will it wake him up?"

"No," Dawn said, returning with Ava at her side. "When we did this with Lori, it was a very short and recent memory we were working with. We have to go further back with Kyle to make sure he's forgotten everything about us. I added a little something extra to make sure he gets a thorough nap. He'll need it anyway, and it'll give us some time to get him the hell out of the packhouse. Come on, Ava. Let's do it."

The two of them arranged themselves near Kyle's head. Ava dabbed a bit of oily liquid from the little vial onto her finger. She slowly rubbed it back and forth across Kyle's forehead, her lips moving as she recited words that Pierce couldn't hear. Her finger made a grid pattern across his skin, slowly gliding back and forth, up and down, until she'd covered his entire forehead.

Dawn sat attentively next to her, listening to Ava and watching the patient. When her niece was done, Dawn pressed her hands on either side of Kyle's head. She closed her eyes and tipped her head back, and a pulsing green light illuminated her palms. It swelled out to her fingertips and radiated over Kyle's skull. The light disappeared when she took her hands away and opened her eyes. She smiled at Ava. "You did it. Great job."

"Thanks," Ava beamed. "I never thought I'd get a chance to actually try it."

"You're talented, sweetheart." Rex held up his palm to give her a high five but spotted the oily residue still on Ava's fingers. "I'll owe you one."

Ava waggled her fingers at him and stuck out her tongue before she headed to the bathroom to wash up.

Pierce turned to Rex. "I'll ask Holly where he was staying, and then we can take him back there."

"Good start, but we'll probably need more than that," Rex suggested. "The guy's just had his memory wiped from the past week. I think we have to create a little backstory for him. Maybe there's some other news story he would've stayed in town to work on. We can print out some information and plant them at his place."

"You're the Alpha." Pierce headed upstairs. He and Holly had hardly spoken to each other on the ride over there. That awkward tension between them had only become more unwieldy with so many of his other packmates surrounding them. He hadn't liked the idea of just leaving her at her place, though.

"Pierce." Joan turned to him as he came up out of the basement and passed through the kitchen. She stood at the stove, just taking a kettle off the burner. The retired Luna of their pack, Joan still served the Glenwoods as a wisewoman and an oracle. She turned to him with a sympathetic look. "How are you doing, dear?"

"I'm fine. I'm just tired. This has been—" he rolled his hand through the air as he tried to think, "—a lot."

"I know." She took his hand between hers, her fingers cool and gentle. "You've got a special connection with that sweet woman outside, don't you?"

Pierce's eyes flicked to the sliding door. He could see Holly out there at a table with several of the Glenwood women. That connection Joan spoke about tugged at him even now, reminding him that even having one wall separating them was too much. "I do."

She nodded. "Perhaps it isn't any of my business, other than the fact that I worry about all of you as though you're my own children. I only wonder if there's anything I can do to help. I know the incident with this journalist has made things difficult, but I think something more is putting a wall between the two of you."

He pulled a deep breath in through his nose. Pierce didn't want to have the mate debate yet again with yet another person. He could tell her about how he and Holly lived on opposite sides of the country and had their own lives. He could tell her that it was simply too late for them and that if things had happened differently, they might be able to work it all out. Instead, his mind wandered to a part of his issue with Holly that he hadn't yet been able to wrap his head around. "There seems to be a lot keeping us apart, but there's one aspect that I honestly don't know how to handle."

"What is it?" Joan asked, eager to help.

"She's not like us," Pierce admitted. "She's a shifter, but she's a bear. If we were able to figure out all of our other differences—which I honestly don't have much hope for—we'd still have that as a problem. I don't mind it, of course. I think she's beautiful. It's just that…I'd want to follow our pack traditions. I don't know what might happen if I were to mark her."

"Ah, I see." Joan's long beaded necklace tinkled softly as she let go of his hand and poured hot water from the kettle into her mug. "Would you like some tea?"

"No, thank you." What he'd like was a magic spell that would've made him meet Holly twenty years earlier, back when they were young and the world still felt malleable.

Joan reached for the jar of honey. "Fate acts in very mysterious ways. It's something we have to think about a lot since it's so closely tied in with our way of life. That doesn't always make it any easier, though, especially when it seems like it's beating the hell out of us."

He let out a grunt of agreement. "It's good at that."

"Yes, it is, but I still think it's acting in our best interests." She slowly stirred her tea and then set the spoon in the sink. "It has a plan for us."

Pierce thought about his mother dying so young and his father's house burning down. He thought about how Holly had been in Eugene once a year for several years, yet he'd never met her until now. Then, even once he did meet her, he wouldn't get a chance to be with her. "Sorry to say it, but this doesn't seem like much of a plan."

"That's because it's much greater than anything we can possibly fathom," Joan explained. "It's bigger than us, much bigger. Our little brains simply can't comprehend something as vast as the way we're all interwoven."

"But has a wolf ever marked another species before?" Pierce pressed, ready to get back down to brass tacks. If the result would be something terrible, there was no point in working out their other issues. "Do you know what might happen?"

"Not from experience, no," the older woman admitted. "Perhaps we could see if there's any other information we can tap into."

Joan reached up and put her warm hands on either side of his face. She smiled up at him as she tipped her head back. Her hazel eyes suddenly went cloudy, and her shoulders slackened. She blinked a moment later, and her eyes returned to their natural color. "Follow your heart."

"What?" Pierce had occasionally experienced Joan's oracular talents before, and he'd been expecting something much more cryptic.

"Follow your heart. Those exact words in that exact order," she confirmed as she dropped her hands to her sides.

He shook his head. "I thought that's what I've been trying to do all along."

She grinned at him. "Then I suggest you keep trying. I'm going to read a bit and then go to bed, but you know where I'm at when you need me."

Joan left him alone, and Pierce headed for the sliding door.

"She wasn't kidding," Angela said. "Sasquatch actually does make his appearances pretty regularly around here. I have to admit I'm pretty amused that Tiffany was able to use him to throw off the scent for the rest of us, though."

"Hey, we've got to do what we can, right?" Stephanie said. Facing the house, she was the first one to see the door open. "Hey, Pierce. Everything going okay?"

"It's mostly taken care of," he replied as he stepped out into the night. "I just need to talk to Holly for a second."

Angela looked at her watch. "And I've got to get home and into bed."

"Same," Stephanie agreed. "I wouldn't have even been out this late if it hadn't been for an emergency call at the office. But I have a long day of doggy acupuncture and massages ahead of me, so I'd better turn in. It was nice to meet you, Holly."

"Thank you. You, too." She waved her fingers at them as they left.

Pierce waited until the door had closed behind them. "Do you mind if I sit down?"

"Not at all." The moon cast her in a gorgeous glow, illuminating her skin and brightening her eyes despite how tired she must have been. "Everyone in your pack is so nice. What's happening with Kyle?"

He settled into the chair next to her. It pleased his wolf to be so close, but it also suited him not to have to look into her eyes for this entire conversation. Nothing between them had been easy, and it didn't seem to be getting any better. "You clocked him good, but he'll be all right physically."

"Physically?" she asked.

Pierce nodded. "Dawn is a very talented woman, as are many in the Glenwood bloodline. She's more than just a skilled nurse. She and Max's daughter Ava were able to wipe his memory. When Kyle wakes up, he won't know a thing about people like us."

"Oh." She chewed her lip for a moment. "That's wild, but it's actually kind of a relief. I didn't know how we were going to stop him."

"We won't have to worry about him now. We just

have a little homework to do." Pierce told her about Rex's suggestion of a new article.

"I'm sure I can come up with something," Holly promised. She folded her hands in her lap and shifted in her seat, looking uncomfortable. "Listen, Pierce. I really am sorry for all of this. I thought I could deal with Kyle on my own and keep our secret from being exposed. I can see now that I should've just told you about it."

"It's all right," he replied. "I know you were just trying to protect me, too."

"Yes, although you seem to need a lot less of that than I do," she remarked.

He smiled despite himself. "I don't know. I saw the way you walloped him."

She turned to face him. "You actually saw it?"

"Through the window," he confirmed. "Next time you shift inside a house, you might want to make sure the curtains are drawn."

"I'll be sure to keep that in mind," she promised with a laugh that quickly dissipated. "Can I tell you something?"

She could tell him everything and anything. As long as they were close to each other and she hadn't yet gotten on a plane for Massachusetts, he would sit and listen. "Sure."

"There's another reason I didn't tell you I was staying in Eugene other than believing I could safeguard you from Kyle."

He licked his lips and waited, not knowing what to expect.

"It was just too hard," she admitted after a moment, her voice thick. "It was too hard to spend time with you when I knew it was so limited. I made excuses to myself that I deserved to have a little fun, but I was really only teasing myself. I knew I'd only fall for you more than I already had, but then I'd have to go home."

Her words poured over him just as the moonlight did. They couldn't fix what'd happened between them, but they were a greater comfort than she could know. "I understand. It was hard for me, too. I guess that's why I was so upset when I found out you were still here. I knew the reality of our situation, but I didn't like thinking that I'd missed out on any time with you. It would be painful later, but I still wanted every second with you that I could get. I still do. I know we're different, but we've got a bond I don't think we can deny at this point."

She looked down at her lap. "Maybe we're not that different, after all."

"You're right. I was also more than ready to clock

Kyle," he replied. It was a serious talk, but he felt a desperate urge to lighten the mood. Once Kyle was taken care of, she'd have no reason to stay. She'd be gone, and he didn't want their last moments together to be so somber.

"I'm sure, but that's not what I mean." Holly picked at the hem of her shirt. "I started to wonder a few days ago when I realized how off I felt. I just didn't feel like myself at all. I wasn't clearheaded, and I wasn't thinking things through. My mind felt completely blocked. I was so quick to anger, and I couldn't control myself. That irresponsible shift of mine that you saw tonight? That's not me. That's not something I would do. I don't think I'd ever hit someone, either."

He leaned forward, turning his head to the side to see her face. "It was a pretty hard night for all of us."

"No. I never would've shifted in front of Kyle if I could help it, but once I did, I knew for sure." Holly looked up. Her throat bobbed as she swallowed, and he thought he saw tears of concern in her eyes. "Pierce, I'm pregnant."

The last bit of air in his lungs drifted out on its own accord. He was glad he was sitting down, or he might've gone crashing straight to the deck. There were many things they needed to discuss, but this wasn't a conversation he'd been imagining he'd have. "You are?"

"And before you ask, I'm sure. I could sense it when I shifted." She twisted her fingers together in her lap and chewed her lip again. "I don't even know what to think about it. I'm forty-three years old. At this point, I hadn't thought I'd ever start a family."

And yet they had. Their one night of passion had been the beginning of an entire life. Joy flushed through his body, mixed with instinctive pride and elation. He wanted to run back into the packhouse and tell everyone. But when he saw how uncertain Holly was about the whole thing, it hollowed him out. "We should talk about this. We'll figure out how to handle it all."

Holly frowned as she swiped at the corner of her eye. "We should, but I don't think I can right now. I need time to process all of this. I need time to even think about what questions I have, if that makes sense."

Dozens of them were already flooding his mind. "It does. We'll figure this out, Holly. I promise."

"How can you be so confident when we haven't managed to figure anything else out yet?" She wiped her face again.

There was nothing he wanted more than to pull her onto his lap, hold her close, and feel her in his arms. He wanted to press his cheek to her head and feel the softness of her hair, to entwine his fingers around her hip and never let her go.

But he'd give her the time she asked for. He'd give her anything. "I just know."

15

Holly polished off her scrambled eggs. She rinsed her plate and then turned to the fridge to see what else she might have. At least now she knew why she was so emotional and wanted to eat so much. It was incredibly early in the pregnancy yet, but she knew from family members that the typical symptoms could start far sooner for people like them.

She cut up a peach and slowly munched it, relishing the bright sweetness on her tongue. Holly thought about calling her sister. She'd told Ivy she'd be staying in Eugene a while longer to work on a project. The project she now had developing inside her wasn't exactly what she'd intended, and that was too much of a conversation to have over the phone.

Hey, sis. I went on a work trip, met my mate, and got knocked up. See you when I get back!

Yeah, that was definitely too much right now. She washed her plates and put them on the drying rack. This little house had been a great place to rent for the past couple of weeks. She was glad that she and Dahlia had been able to have a little more privacy there instead of getting a hotel room, but it couldn't last forever. She'd only been able to extend her stay for an extra week before the next renters had booked the place, and it was time to move on.

If only she knew how to do that.

Holly stepped into the living room, which she'd been avoiding since the night before, other than to walk through it to get somewhere else. She picked up the lamp she'd knocked over and swept up the glass from the bulb. "That's what I get for swinging my big bear butt around."

Her bear had been talking to her a lot lately. It wanted to be with its mate. It didn't care about any of the finer details that went into a decision like that. Her child deserved its father, and Pierce deserved a chance to be that father. But Holly knew she couldn't pick up her whole life and move it there. Eugene was nice, but it was so far from her home and family.

She'd have Pierce and the Glenwood wolves but still feel like something was missing. It just wasn't right.

Somehow, in the chaos of the evening, a side table had fallen over. Holly put it back to rights, wondering how long she should be lifting things like that in her condition. Then again, did those restrictions apply to shifters or only humans? The first person she thought to ask was Dawn, and that thought created a flood of other questions. She was too old for this. She'd already established her life and her home. Now, she would have a little one. Though her cheeks warmed at the idea of a chubby little face smiling up at her, she knew it wouldn't be easy. Holly rubbed a hand over her stomach, which was gently curved only because her metabolism wasn't what it used to be. What about the pregnancy itself? How was she going to get through it?

Tears burned the backs of her eyes. She blinked them away and gritted her teeth, determined not to cry. She wouldn't be able to stop, she knew. Yes, she was on the older side for this. But she was also a mature, smart woman. She'd get it figured out. Somehow.

The knock at the door startled her. Holly cursed under her breath for being so fidgety and hurried to answer it. She inhaled when she saw Pierce standing on the porch.

He was dressed in a button-down shirt and nice jeans, holding a giant bouquet of roses in front of him. "Good morning."

"Ah, good morning." She opened the door further to let him in. Her bear was full of ecstasy, both from the sweet scent of the flowers that filled the air and seeing its mate. He was there, and she needed him to be. After all, he was just as much a part of this pregnancy as she was. The other side of her wanted to proceed with caution. Judging by his freshly shaven face and those over-the-top roses, Pierce definitely had a plan in mind. "I don't know if I have a vase."

"That's okay." He laid the flowers gently on the coffee table, reached for her hand, and guided her to the couch.

She sat, still tired from all the events that'd led up to this moment. Pierce had dropped her off at her place in the early morning hours once everything settled down at the packhouse. She'd tossed and turned for a short while before getting up, but he looked as bright and fresh as if he'd slept all night. "I didn't expect to see you so soon."

"I know." He sat beside her on the couch and

boldly took her hand in his, bringing it onto his lap and holding it securely. "I know you said you weren't ready to talk yet. I understand, and my intention isn't to go against that. I only ask that you listen. You don't have to say anything, okay?"

Her throat tightened with nerves, but her curiosity was piqued. "Okay."

"Holly, I know none of the decisions ahead of us are small ones. I get that you wanted some time to think. I figured I needed to do the same, but it didn't take long to realize I didn't have to think at all." He turned away and laughed lightly. "Sorry. I can hear that I'm starting to ramble."

"Don't worry about it. My thoughts have been nothing but wild rambles lately."

Pierce cleared his throat and tried again. "What I'm trying to say is that it doesn't take any thought for me to know that I want to be with you. That was true when we first met, and it's still true now that we're going to have a baby. You're my mate, and my wolf and soul have never been happier than when we've been together. We'll have some challenges, but we've already had to deal with a big one. We can figure this out together, but we can't do it living thousands of miles apart."

She nodded, waiting. The same feeling she

would've gotten if she'd stepped up to a cliff rose inside her chest.

"I'm inviting you to stay, Holly, right here in Eugene with me. You work from home, and your company headquarters is right here anyway. My place is a bit cramped right now with my dad staying there, but it won't be that way forever. We'll find a new house for him when his insurance money comes in, and then we'll have the guest room for the baby."

"Oh, Pierce." She backed away from the cliff in her mind, knowing it was a leap she simply couldn't take. "It's very sweet of you, and I love that you went to the trouble of figuring out how it would work, but it just won't. I don't belong here. I don't know why. It's a great place, and it's nice to visit, but it's just not for me. I don't think I can be happy this far away from my clan and my home. I'm sorry."

"That's okay." A slight smile remained on his face despite the rejection, and he didn't even seem surprised. "There's another option. I'll go with you."

Her shoulders sagged. Her lips parted, but no words came out. Holly could hardly believe what she was hearing. "Are you serious?"

"Yes. I don't know enough about your life back in Cape Cod to say much about how we'll live or where

I'll work. Even without those details, I've never been more serious about anything in my life."

She gripped his hand in hers. "Pierce, that's such a generous offer. I can't say I haven't entertained the idea myself, but I couldn't fathom taking you away from your family. I want you to be really sure."

"I am." He pulled her hand up and pressed it against his chest. "I've been watching my fellow pack members find their mates, wondering when and if it would ever happen to me. Now it is, and I can't just let you slip away."

It was too good to be true. "Won't you miss everything here?"

"Yeah." A twinge of pain wrinkled his brow, but only for a moment. "There will be things I'll miss, but not as much as I'd miss you if you left."

"Wow." She'd blown him away with her shocking news the night before, and now he was returning the favor. "I never expected that. I just figured you had so much going on here that you couldn't leave."

"If you'd asked me about it a week ago, or maybe even yesterday, you would've been right. I didn't think I could possibly leave. My whole life and everything I've ever known is here." His dark blue eyes looked deeply into hers, making her feel like there was nothing else he wanted to see in the entire world. "Did you get to meet Joan last night? She's our pack oracle, and I asked her about us. She told me to follow my heart and emphasized that the words themselves were really important. I know why now. You're my heart, and I'll follow you anywhere."

"Pierce." The tears she'd tried to stop earlier now flowed freely, touched by his sweet words. "You really want to do this, don't you?"

"Yes, for both you and the baby. I don't want to be a part-time father. I just want to be with you if you'll have me." He brought up his other hand and held them both against hers, his heart pounding through his shirt.

Her heart picked up the beat and echoed its rhythm. It was so easy to imagine the two of them together back home, and she knew they could be happy that way. "I will. I definitely will." She leaned in and kissed him, feeling the softness of his lips and the heat of his mouth. Her soul surged toward him, finally happy now that everything would truly be all right.

"There's something else I wanted to ask you about," he said when they parted. "I mentioned it briefly before, but it's my pack's tradition to mark our mates."

Holly had heard of the custom. She knew about

the ceremonial bite, but she'd never known anyone who'd actually experienced it. "Yeah, I remember."

"I know it's old-fashioned, but it's something that brings mates that much closer together. That's actually what I was asking Joan about last night." He looked at their entwined hands and then bent his head to kiss the back of her fingers.

"Why?"

"Because I don't know how it'll work," he explained. "We know what it's like when a wolf marks another wolf, and that connection deepens. When a wolf bites a human, it makes her become like him. You're a shifter, but you're not a wolf."

"I see." She sat back a little while she thought about this. Holly had seen him in his wolf form. He was strong and handsome, and his teeth looked incredibly sharp. It wouldn't take much for them to sink straight through her flesh. She already had a beast that lived inside her, though. "Do you think it'd be any danger to the baby?"

"I don't know for sure," he admitted. "The child already has half my blood, though."

"That's true." A warm sensation moved through her, knowing she was creating a life that was a part of each of them, concrete evidence of their bond.

Pierce reached up and swept a strand of her hair

away from her face. "Like I said, this is what I was asking Joan about. The message about following my heart had to do with you, but also with this."

They had very little information to go on. Her instincts were trying to guide her. She'd been resisting them ever since Pierce had come into her life, telling herself they could never change themselves enough to be together. Maybe it was time to start listening to her heart and inner bear. It knew what it wanted, even if it sounded scary. "I suppose no one will ever know for sure until it happens."

The tip of his tongue escaped his lips as he ran it across his teeth. "We could always wait until after the baby is born."

"No." The word came not from her lips or tongue but from her very spirit. "I don't want to wait. I've already waited a long time to find you, and then I almost left town without any guarantee that I'd see you again. I love you, Pierce, and anything we can do to be together has got to be right."

"I love you, too, Holly." He pulled her in close and kissed her again, his lips raking across hers and his arms closing around her. Pierce's strong hands scooped around her and brought her easily up onto his lap, and she melted against his body.

Her lips parted and their tongues entwined, and

Holly knew everything about this was right. She'd always loved him, and they wouldn't let anything else stand in their way. There was no time for wondering and worrying when everything they needed was right there between them.

Pierce's lips wandered down the side of her neck. His hand rose up her back until his fingers found the collar of her shirt, and he gently pulled it aside. Holly leaned her head away, opening herself up to what was to come. They had no idea how it would turn out, but it was an adventure they'd have together. Excitement surged through her body as Pierce pressed kisses to the curve of her neck and slowly moved to just the right spot. Already, she could feel his wolf teeth grazing her, and she closed her eyes and relaxed.

His left hand held her against him, his thumb rubbing small circles against her lower back. A warm breath of air moved over her shoulder as he opened his mouth.

She gasped as his teeth sank in, air catching in her throat at the sudden shock of pain after such sweetness. Holly gripped his shoulders, hanging on as the pain erupted. It intensified as he increased the pressure of his bite to ensure the mark took.

Pierce lifted his teeth from her flesh and kissed

her wounded skin. "I'm sorry," he whispered as he tended to her injury with his mouth. "I know that had to hurt."

"It's okay." She laid her forehead against his shoulder and pressed her face into the curve of his neck, inhaling the scent of his cologne and soaking in the warmth and strength of his body. "I knew it would, but I wanted it. And do you know what else I want?"

His hands roved over her back, pressing on either side of her spine, rubbing in wide circles near her shoulder blades, and moving down to massage her behind. "Hm?"

It was strange to admit. She hadn't imagined she'd feel this way, not when she'd just agreed to a purposeful injury, but the very act of the mark itself had already brought her closer to her mate. "You."

16

With her blood fresh on his lips and her words in his ears, Pierce felt his wolf rallying hard inside him. It'd already been simmering just under his skin, intoxicated by the act of marking his mate. He'd felt the pain inside her as he'd bitten into her flesh. He hadn't wanted to hurt her, but he knew this wasn't like any other injury. It was a symbol of her trust in him and her promise to be with him forever.

There was just one part of the ritual left.

Pierce scooped her up and stood, not once letting her feet touch the ground as he carried her to the bedroom. He took his time, knowing now that they weren't working on a deadline. Holly would still be packing up her things and leaving Eugene behind, but she'd be bringing him with her.

He nuzzled her neck as he reached her bed and slowly let go, letting her body slide down against his until she was on her knees on the mattress. He swept her hair back from her shoulders and ran his hands through it. He would get to enjoy those silky locks for the rest of his life. It was hard to imagine, but only because she made him feel so young and vibrant. It might have taken half his life to find her, but being with her was like getting to start life all over again.

He kissed her forehead, his fingers stroking the angle of her jaw and the smoothness of her throat. "I can't believe I almost let you go."

"You're not the only one." She wrapped her arms around him and laid her head on his chest, holding him tightly. "I guess our stubborn natures were the first thing we had in common."

Pierce laughed. "I have a feeling we're only going to find more as we go along."

She smoothed her hands down the front of his shirt until she reached the bottom. "Yeah? Like what?"

"Hm. Like long walks on the beach?" he ducked his head as she pulled his shirt over it.

Holly tossed it aside and glided her hands across

his bare skin. "Have you ever taken a long walk on the beach?"

"No," he admitted as he started on the buttons of her sleeveless blouse. She'd already left the first few undone, offering him a tantalizing triangle of skin. "I figure I'm about to get plenty of chances, though."

"That's true." Her fingers gripped the top button of his jeans. "What we have in common could also be things we *don't* like, right?"

Pierce chewed the inside of his lip as he tried to work the tiny pearl button back through the hole. How could a flimsy piece of fabric be so effective at keeping him from his mate? "If I'm with you, there won't be much I don't like."

"No?" Holly grunted as she struggled with his fly. "Not even all these damn buttons we seem to be wearing?"

He laughed and gently batted her hands away from his jeans, parting the rest of his fly easily. "These aren't difficult."

"Neither are these." Holly demonstrated by effortlessly undoing the row of buttons to reveal her white cotton beneath.

It was practical, not the lacey number she'd worn the last time they'd been together, but Pierce liked it just as much. It gently cradled her breasts above her soft stomach, a scene that reminded him of just how lucky of a man he was. "I guess that just means we make a great team."

"Definitely." Holly slid her hands down inside his loosened jeans and over his ass, sliding the denim down as she caressed the outside of his legs. Her fingers skimmed just above his knees before twisting around and roving up the insides of his thighs. She continued upward, skimming her palm over the bulge in his boxers.

She was doing a good job of distracting him from his original mission of worshipping every square inch of her body. He made quick work of her khaki shorts, which forced her to sit on the edge of the bed so he could pull them over her ankles. She started to get back up when he was done, and he used her motion to pick her up and turn her around so that she was once again sitting on his lap. It was the same position they'd had on the couch, but now there was far less between them.

Holly squealed with surprise. "What are we doing?"

"Just getting comfortable." Pierce ran his hands up her back until he could touch her hair. "Work for you?"

Holly wiggled her hips until she descended on

his hard shaft, slowly enveloping him in such exquisite pleasure that Pierce had to close his eyes. Her thighs closed around him, her feet pressed against his legs. "God, yes."

He slipped his fingers under the band of her bra and pulled it off. Her generous breasts pressed into him, and he knew he could—and willingly would—lose himself in her.

He grabbed her hips, which had become one of his favorite things to do. Pierce would take any excuse to touch this woman he was fortunate enough to call his mate. He held her against him tightly. "I just want to feel you for a moment, just like this."

Holly rested her forehead against his, her hands rubbing up and down his back. It was utter perfection. Pierce knew they'd find many ways they liked being together. It would adjust as her pregnancy advanced, and no doubt they'd have to adjust again once the little one came along, but he knew they'd always have what they were experiencing right now, a sense of peace and pure happiness as a result of their bond.

Eventually, his hips began to rock. Holly swayed in unison, their bodies reading and feeding off each other. Their union before had been hot and feverish, a demand for flesh. Now, it was deep and slow, a heady sweetness like a sultry summer afternoon. Her body shifted against his, and a gentle moan sounded in her throat as her core began to shiver around him.

His breath quickened. Holly threw her head back, grinding her hips harder against him. Pierce felt his entire existence flooding toward her as the heat rose between them.

She cried out, her rapid pulses bringing him right along with her. He panted as his body took full control and Holly shivered against him. Their true bond was complete.

They moved back onto the pillows and Pierce pulled her close, threading his arm around her shoulders and tucking her up close against his side. Would there ever be anything as glorious as lying next to her, with the length of her naked body against his? He'd happily spend his whole life finding out. "You know, I thought I was satisfied after the last time."

She laughed, a vibration against his chest. "Were you not?"

"Not compared to this." He kissed the top of her head. "Not when I know that I get to keep you afterward."

"Mm, yes." She snuggled deeper in against his side. "Have I told you how sweet you are?"

"Possibly, but I'll let you do it again." He rubbed his fingers along her side, reveling in the curves of her body and knowing that she was only going to get curvier over the next few months. Blood rushed to his groin, but he didn't want to disturb this peaceful, dreamy moment. They'd experienced so much chaos in the short time they'd known each other, and they both deserved a minute to relax. "Are you looking forward to going back home?"

"I think it'll be even more of a home once you're there with me, so yes. Also, my mattress is far more comfortable than this one." She wriggled again.

They could've been lying on a park bench and he would've been happy, just as long as they were together. "I guess you'll have to take off a star when you leave a review, huh?"

"No, I can't complain too much since they let me stay an extra week." Holly pushed herself up on her elbows and rolled over to look at him. "I haven't had a whole lot of time to think about what it'll be like to work with a baby, but I'm grateful that I already have a remote position. It means that I'll be able to have him or her with me most of the time, and we'll just need a sitter when I have to go out for longer trips."

Pierce smiled, pleased to know she was starting to think about how well this could work. It was only yesterday that everything felt impossible. "I'll look later today and see if the fire department out there has any openings."

"Going to go ahead and get started?"

"I'm ready to dive in with both feet. Speaking of, am I going to have to pull you out of the ocean all the time once we're out there? Or do you only like to drown in rivers?"

She playfully smacked his chest before curling up under his arm again and pressing her cheek against him. "You're terrible."

"And just a moment ago, you told me how sweet I was," he reminded her, grinning.

"I guess that means you can be both." Holly laid her hand on his chest and ran her fingers slowly through the fine smattering of hair there. "You sure you're not going to miss living here?"

It was something he'd asked himself the previous night—or rather, in the early hours of the morning—after he'd dropped her off and gone back home. The answer had come to him quickly. "I've never lived anywhere else, but I think it's time I did. I like my job, but it's still just a job. I can get one anywhere. You've seen my apartment; it's nothing special. My family is here, but I can come back and visit. You're what I'd miss the most if I stayed."

"And now I get the sweet version of you again," she mumbled. Her breathing was getting slower, and she leaned more heavily on him.

She had to be exhausted. Now that they were safe and happy together, Pierce felt some of that exhaustion draping over him, too. It'd been a very long night, and he hadn't slept at all. Pierce yawned, though his mind was still working over the logistics of his impending move. "I think the only thing I'll feel sad about leaving behind is my dad. He can take over my apartment, so that's easy enough, but I feel bad for him. He lost the house he'd spent pretty much his entire adult life in. The insurance money will come through, but it won't feel the same."

"He should just come live with us."

Pierce was suddenly awake again. "Do you mean that?"

"Yeah, if you think he'd want to." She rolled again so that she lay on her back. "My house isn't huge, but there's an apartment over the garage. It needs a little fixing up. I was going to rent it out, but I'd never gotten around to getting it all done."

The idea was getting him even more excited about the move. It would be good for Rick to get out of this town full of memories and create some new ones. "I'm sure he wouldn't need to live with us for very long, and then he could find a new place of his own."

When she shook her head, her hair rubbed softly against his skin. "Why? He could just stay there, and then we'd have help with the baby. I think it'd be kind of nice."

"Me, too." Pierce grazed his fingers over her arm as he leaned against the pillow and thought about it. Holly already had family and friends out in Massachusetts. He only had her, but he could have his father, too. "I'll ask him about it today."

She didn't respond.

Pierce waited a moment and then realized she'd fallen asleep. She needed it, and he was content to hold her until she woke up again. Everything else in the world could wait. He craned his neck so he could see her face, soft and gentle as she rested. Would their child look like her, with her wide eyes and slim face? Would its eyes be soft gray like hers or dark blue like his? Would it be a bear or a wolf? He didn't care one way or another, just as long as it was happy and healthy.

17

Pierce walked into the guest bedroom, checking the closet and behind the door. He moved into the bedroom that had been his own for the last five years, once he'd moved out of a tinier apartment and thought he might like a little extra space. It looked smaller without the king-sized bed and dresser taking up most of the floor. He retrieved a tie tack that'd probably fallen out of a drawer when it was being moved out.

"Everything is good on this side," he said as he headed into the empty living room. His voice echoed as he looked in the kitchen. "How about in there?"

"Just an expired box of cake mix that got left in the back of the cabinet," she announced as she closed the cabinet door. "I didn't know you like to bake."

"I don't, which is exactly why it's expired," he quipped.

Holly pitched the box into the trash can, the only thing remaining in the apartment. "Lucky for you, I do like to bake every now and then."

"What kind of confectionery delights do I have to look forward to?" Pierce asked as he tied up the trash bag and lifted it out of the can.

"Nothing crazy," she replied. "Just cookies and muffins. Maybe some brownies."

"So you're good in the kitchen, at the keyboard, *and* in bed. I definitely scored." He winked at her and dodged out the door, where she wouldn't have a chance to give him too much of a retort without potentially being overheard by their neighbors.

"It's going to be a long drive to Massachusetts, isn't it?"

Pierce made sure the door was locked before they headed down the stairs. "Definitely."

"Go to your left. No, your other left. There. Perfect." Rick put down his end of the dresser on the back of the moving van and then came around to help Jack push it in place. "Great job, buddy."

"I've had a little experience with it lately," Jack replied. "Are you going to come back and see us?"

"Of course," his grandfather replied. "And you'll have to come out to Cape Cod to see us."

"Do you think I can get Dad away from the firehouse long enough to do that?" Jack challenged.

"Not now that he's going to be the new chief," Pierce said as they walked up. He handed Jack a fifty-dollar bill. "Thanks for all your help."

Rick held out his hand. "Where's my share?"

"You'll get it after we unload this thing on the other end of the line," Pierce reminded him. "I think free housing just off the beach is payment enough."

"Hmm." Rick drummed his fingers on his jaw as he pretended to think. "Yeah, I guess you're right."

"We'd better get going," Holly said as she checked her watch. "Lori said they should have everything ready by noon."

Pierce turned to his mate. She'd been working just as hard as he had over the past week to make sure everything was packed up and ready to go. She hadn't had to do any of the heavy lifting, of course, but being away from home for three weeks on top of being pregnant had to be taking its toll on her. "Are you sure you're up for it?"

"I'm fine," she assured him. "There's no way we're going to miss our chance to say goodbye to everyone, even if it's also saying hello to some of them on my part. Honestly, nothing sounds better right now than sitting in a lawn chair and putting my feet up while I have a grilled burger and some potato chips."

"Yessss," Jack agreed. He turned and trotted toward the cab of the moving van. "I'm riding with you, Grandpa!"

Pierce and Holly got in his truck and drove out to the Glenwood packhouse one last time. It was a familiar drive, one he could make from any part of town without having to think about it. He felt a little wistful knowing he'd never be making it again, but he knew it would soon be replaced with a new drive as he got to know his new home. Adjustments would have to be made for both of them, but he knew it'd all be worth it.

"There they are! The couple of the hour!" Rex said as they pulled into the driveway of the Glenwood packhouse. He opened Holly's door and held out his arm. "My lady."

"Thank you." Holly flushed as she took his arm and stepped down.

"Pierce." Lori came to his side of the truck and greeted him with a kiss on the cheek. "We're all so happy for the two of you, but we're going to miss you so much."

"I don't know if we're worth all of this," Pierce said as the Alpha and Luna escorted them around to the back of the house. The deck and yard were swarming with Glenwoods. Two grills were up and running, and numerous coolers held drinks. Three long folding tables had been set up to hold all the food and desserts. Children played in the sprinkler or tossed around a ball. It was a beautiful sight, making him realize how much he meant to the pack.

"Holly!" Dawn rushed up to give her new friend a hug. "It's not fair, you know. Just as I get to know you, it's time for you to leave."

"I'm sure we'll be back," Holly assured her. "I don't think I can keep him away from you guys forever."

"That's true. Or maybe we'll just rent a charter bus and bring the whole pack out to you. We could all use a vacation," she laughed.

"I don't think I can fit you into my house, but there's room at our clanhouse," Holly agreed.

"You call me if you have any questions about that baby," Dawn ordered.

Gage, Dawn's mate, reached out for Pierce's hand. "Congratulations on everything. It's all going to change when you have that little one, but only for the better."

"Tell me how you want your burgers done," Kane called from the grill.

His cousin Bennett stepped up beside him and looked at what he was doing. "Looks like you're just burning them all, anyway."

The police officer gave him the side eye. "It's called a char, thank you very much. It's what brings out the flavor."

"It's what makes it a hockey puck instead of a delicious, juicy burger," Bennett retorted. "Give me that spatula. I'll show you how it's done."

Their mates, Stephanie and Melissa, giggled nearby. "Maybe it's a good thing you're getting Pierce away from his brother, Holly," Melissa said. "Otherwise, you'd have to listen to stuff like this all the time."

Kane playfully stuck out his lower lip. "Hey, now. We're not that bad."

Melissa winked at him. "I guess you're tolerable."

"None of you are." Max walked up with Sarah at his side, and more hugs went all around. "Holly, I don't think I've officially said it yet, but thank you for what you did to protect our pack."

Holly shook her head. She was only a couple of

weeks pregnant, but already Pierce could swear he spotted the glow of motherhood on her cheeks. "You really can't thank me when you guys were the ones who did all the work."

"Don't shortchange yourself," Sarah argued. "If you hadn't done everything you did, we might never have found out about Kyle's little project in the first place. You were pretty courageous, and I heard you were the one who actually clobbered him."

"That's not the kind of thing I usually do," Holly said, tenting her fingers against her forehead in embarrassment.

Max shook his head. "That's too bad because Pierce here might need a good clobbering every now and then."

"What? Who's clobbering who? I want in on the action," Brody said as he approached. He carried his daughter Evelyn on his hip.

Her strawberry blonde hair had been pulled up into two short pigtails and her big hazel eyes peeked out under a fringe of bangs. She reached out to grab the fist that Brody had playfully put up in the air. "No, Daddy. No fighting."

"No?" Brody asked.

Evelyn pressed her lips and emphatically shook her head. "No."

"Okay, then. Whatever you say. Do you want to go play with your cousins?" Brody put her down when she started wiggling and watched her run off toward the other children. "There you go, Pierce. A sneak peek into your future. Your whole world will be commanded by a tiny shifter."

"I'm looking forward to it," Pierce promised as he pulled Holly close. It'd been a sheer joy for him to share their good news with all the Glenwoods, and that joy only grew as everyone else seemed to share in it.

Robin slipped her hand into Brody's and beamed at the happy couple. "I think Joan and Jimmy wanted a chance to talk to you two. They're up on the deck."

"Sure thing." He guided Holly up toward the house. "Are you doing okay?"

"Do I look that terrible?" she asked with a laugh.

"I'm sorry. I just worry about you. You mean the world to me, and it took half of my life to find you. I want to make sure you're as happy as possible." He knew he sounded mushy, and his brother would probably make fun of him if he had the chance, but Pierce didn't care. "You've had to meet a lot of new people in a really short amount of time, and there's no shortage of personalities around here."

"Trust me, it probably won't be any different when we get home," she promised, brushing her hair behind her. The mark on her shoulder had left the faintest scar, which peeked out from under the boatneck collar of her top. "I've already given the good news to my sister and parents, and they've been blowing up my phone with plans and questions. Our roles will be reversed when we get home, and then I'll get to ask you if you're all right."

Pierce bent down to plant a kiss on her forehead. "I will be."

"There's still something wrong with the transmission," Jimmy was saying as they stepped up onto the deck. "I know I'll get it eventually, and then it'll be ready to go."

"You'll have to forget about your cars for a moment," Joan said as she spotted the new couple. "Our guests of honor are here."

"Ah, the happy couple!" Jimmy said as he got to his feet. "We're sad to see you go, but I wanted you to both know that you'll always be a part of our pack, no matter where you're at."

"Don't you think it's Rex's job to tell him that?" his mate asked with a smile.

Jimmy shrugged. "Once an Alpha, always an Alpha. Besides, I know for a fact that he feels the same way. I'm sorry we didn't have more of a chance to get to know you, Holly, but we'll be looking for all your future articles."

"That's very sweet of you, but please don't feel like you have to do that just for my sake."

Joan laughed. "Don't discourage him! It's about time he got his nose out from under a hood for more than five minutes and actually read a few paragraphs."

Jimmy turned his bright blue eyes on her. "As I recall, it was my car that first got your attention."

"Oh, Jimmy..."

"It's true," the old man said to Pierce with a wink. "I knew how to rev her engine."

Joan was trying to hold herself together and be polite, but she burst into another round of laughter. "And he still does! I guess that's our little tidbit of advice for you two before you leave us: you're never too old to enjoy each other."

"We'll keep that in mind."

"If the happy couple is looking for advice," a deep voice said from over his shoulder, "it would be to spend as much time together as you possibly can."

"Declan! It's good to see you. I wasn't sure when you guys were going out on tour again." Pierce introduced his mate to the rather famous Declan Ridgefield, lead singer of Wildwood, and his mate Tiffany.

"Actually, we've met before," Tiffany replied.

Holly had blushed at meeting a celebrity like Declan, but her countenance quickly turned to one of horror. "I am *so* very sorry about that. I was trying my best to get him to shut up, but he's pretty good at opening his mouth and sticking his foot straight in it."

"I could tell," Tiffany said with a laugh. "And don't worry. I could tell just how much he was embarrassing you. Looking back, I should've figured out what he was hoping I'd tell him. You and I could've teamed up and scared the shit out of him."

"That would've saved me a lot of time," Holly admitted. "I have to tell you, your food was delicious! We'll be sure to come in every time we return to Eugene."

Declan clapped Pierce on the shoulder. "Hey, I'm just glad to know you'll be coming back. And there's always a chance you might see us. Now that Tiffany's daughter Hailey is doing better and her twins are living with her full-time again, the band and I are talking about extending our touring season. Just a little," he added quickly at a look from his mate.

"Be sure to look us up if you're in the area,"

Pierce reminded him. "You could always take the ferry over if you play in Boston."

They continued to make their rounds through the party, checking in on Hunter's college studies and thanking Ava again for her help in wiping Kyle's memory. Conner had brought his mate McKenzie, and the two of them seemed to be just as in love as they had when he'd first brought her to the packhouse. Stephanie's daughter Annie had a mate now, as well, a young man who watched her every move with wide puppy dog eyes.

"I have to admit I'm a little jealous of them," Pierce said quietly to Holly when they had a moment alone and their plates loaded with food.

She polished off her burger. "Why is that?"

"Because finding their mates so early means they get to spend that much more time with them," he explained, poking a potato chip into a bit of dip. "I wish I'd found you a long time ago."

"I know. I've thought about that, too." She rolled her eyes up toward the trees, looking thoughtful. "I like to think there's a reason, though. If we already had difficulty getting together now, maybe it would've been even harder for us back then."

He shook his head. "I don't know. I was a pretty

determined guy back then. I'll bet we wouldn't have been able to keep our hands off each other."

"We still can't," she reminded him as she reached over and rubbed his leg.

They spent a few moments chatting with Caleb and Jennifer. Sean and Angela had arrived just then and joined them, and Tammy had even managed to bring Carter to the party. Pierce could see just how well Holly was getting along with his pack. It made him a little sad to know they'd be leaving, but it also meant they'd always have a place to come home to.

The light was shifting, and Pierce could feel the change reflecting within him. He was feeling a little wistful, but it was nothing compared to the excitement that rippled through him for this new adventure. "I think it's about time for us to hit the road."

"Not before you say goodbye to us." Hayden grabbed his little brother by the back of the neck.

"I won't miss that," Pierce cracked before he punched Hayden in the arm. "You sure you're cut out to be the new fire chief? It's a lot of responsibility."

"Definitely," Hayden assured him, "although I wasn't expecting it."

"You should've," Rick said as he walked up. He'd snagged another hot dog from Kane before he burned it to a crisp. "You only had the best two references in the world."

"What about you?" Jessica asked her father-in-law. "What are you going to do with all your free time?"

"There's no such thing as free time," Rick replied. "I'll have plenty to do, first with getting everything moved into Holly's place and then fixing up the apartment over the garage."

Holly shook her head. "I never meant that you had to do all the work yourself."

He waved away her words. "I've been a homeowner for over forty years, so I know a thing or two. Besides, I've always wanted to try my hand at a bit of carpentry. You know I'll do a decent job because I'm the one who has to live with it. I'm on a bit of a time crunch, though. I want all that out of the way before the baby comes along. Then it's time to switch into full Grandpa mode."

Pierce ran his hand over his mouth to suppress a laugh. His father had always been energetic, but he could tell the old man was even more enthusiastic than usual. This move was getting him excited, too. It really was just what they all needed.

Rick yelped as Verna stepped up behind him and smacked his ass. "You're going have all those women in Cape Cod in a tizzy. They're used to old geezers who sit around and watch television all day, so they'll be falling all over themselves when you show up and start swinging tools around."

"Trust me, I'm not interested in any of that," Rick said, turning so that his backside no longer faced her.

As Rick and Verna carried on and Jessica and Holly cried over how much they'd come to like each other, Hayden pulled Pierce aside. "Hey, I just wanted to wish you good luck. Not that I think you're going to need it. The two of you are pretty good together, and I'm glad you've found her."

"Yeah, me too." Pierce turned to look at Holly, who was now hugging all of Hayden and Jessica's kids as well, telling them to come out for a vacation and how they could spend all week on the beach. "I think she's going to be a great mom."

"And you'll be a good dad, but don't be afraid to call me for advice," Hayden reminded him with a grin. "I've got three of them, so one of them is after me for something at pretty much any given time. I've got some good secrets that even Rick Westbrook probably hasn't thought of."

"I'll need them because I'm sure Dad is going to spoil the hell out of our little one. You sure you don't mind us taking him away like this?" Pierce was happy to have his father along for the move. It meant a lot to him that it was Holly's idea, that she wanted him there just as much as Pierce did. He still worried that he might be depriving Hayden or his kids by taking him all the way to the other side of the country, though.

"We'll miss him, of course, but it'll be a good excuse for us to take a good trip. Honestly, I think he needs this. If he stays here, he's just going to think about everything he's lost. All he can do out there in New England is gain new memories and new family," Hayden theorized.

Pierce nodded. "He'd hate it if he knew we were standing around planning his life out for him."

His brother grinned. "All the more reason to do it."

"I know those looks," Rick said once Verna had gone off to visit with Joan. "The two of you are up to something."

"Always," Pierce promised. "Are you ready to go?"

With one more round of hugs under their belt, Pierce and Holly got in the truck and Rick hopped up into the moving van. They rolled down the windows and waved until the packhouse was just a tiny speck in the distance.

EPILOGUE

Holly tapped out the last words of her article and sat back, stretching her arms as she looked out the window. The second-story room she'd converted into an office when she'd bought the house was the perfect place to work. The long dormer with its row of windows offered a stunning view of the bay and brought in tons of natural light. She gazed out at the white puffy clouds that drifted by, stained orange by the setting sun.

A ping on her computer brought her back to her work. It was a company-wide email from Marshall Newman discussing the annual meeting that would be coming up in about a month. She and Pierce would have the perfect excuse to head back to

Eugene, and this was bound to be the first annual meeting she truly enjoyed.

Scrolling further down, she spotted a photo of Kyle Freeman. His hair was still the shocking white it'd been when she'd last seen him. Everyone in the company knew about it and whispered speculations about what had happened, but Kyle had never opened his mouth. Marshall proudly boasted about Kyle's article making the front page of not only one of Newman Media's papers but also a nationally recognized paper. He'd been working on an expose of a large corporation near Portland that was covering up their environmental transgressions, and Marshall was excited to announce it was getting such massive attention.

Apparently, the information they'd planted in his hotel room on that fateful night had been more valuable than she or the Glenwoods could've imagined.

A cry sounded on the floor below her. Holly was instantly out of her chair and heading for the door. She even surprised herself sometimes with just how quickly she could react when she knew that little Ruby needed her.

The front door closed before she could get down the stairs. "I've got her. You can go back to work."

"It's all right." She managed to land a quick peck

on Pierce's cheek before he headed down the hall to the nursery. "I'm finished, and dinner should be done."

"Dinner?" The back door slid open, admitting Rick. Holly's cousin Dylan, the Alpha of the Brigham clan, was on his heels. "I could use some dinner after that jog on the beach."

Holly lifted the lid off the slow cooker. Grabbing a cutting board and utensils, she lifted the chicken breasts out of the pot and began shredding them for barbecue sandwiches. "Dylan, you're not wearing him out, are you? He's got plenty of work to do around here," Holly teased.

Dylan took off his hat and swept a hand through his thick, dark hair. He set his hat on the breakfast bar with the Cape Cod National Seashore logo showing. "I think he's got more energy than I do. He can sure keep up, even when we get into the rougher spots where most people don't go."

"I told you he'd be a great guide," Holly told her father-in-law. "I'm glad you're finding plenty around here to do, although I hope you're not overdoing it."

Rick edged around her in the kitchen so he could wash his hands. "Never. My father always said you can sleep when you're dead. I'm not going to say that was exactly accurate, but I can understand the sentiment."

Pierce stepped into the room with a sleepy Ruby in his arms. Her dark hair was in fuzzy tufts where she'd rubbed against her sheets during her nap, and she blinked sleepily at the family standing around her. "Maybe so, but you still could've actually retired like you said you were going to do."

"Are you trying to tell me you don't like serving on the fire department with me?" Rick asked with a grin. He dried his hands and reached his arms out. "Let me have that sweet baby!"

Ruby happily went into his arms, snuggling against her grandpa's chest.

"I'm just giving you hell," Pierce admitted. He brushed his hands across Holly's back. "What can I do to help?"

"I need the sauce from the fridge, and you can get the buns out."

Pierce opened the fridge door. "No, Dad, the only thing I want to know about your job is how you have time for it. You've still got several projects going on in the apartment, and you're always here to help with Ruby anytime we need it. You've been out on the beach or working in the yard. Adding a job to that doesn't sound like much of a retirement."

"Don't forget all the energy he expends fending off the local women," Dylan added. "I used to think jogging along the beach would be a great way for me to find the right one, but they're all too busy looking at him."

Pierce grinned. "It's the same way every time we go out on fire calls. We show up and battle the blaze, then this guy takes his helmet off and they're all shocked at the gray hair. He's had more than one of them try to slip them his number. Or worse, they give *me* their numbers to give to him."

Rick gave both of the other men a scolding look as he cradled his granddaughter in his arms. "It's not like that."

Holly smiled as she put the chicken back in the crock and added the sauce, stirring it to warm it up. "I'm sorry, Rick, but they're right. I can't take you in the grocery store with me anymore."

"What are you talking about?" he asked indignantly.

She laughed. "Don't you remember what happened last week? That woman at the register had her eye on you the moment we got in line. She chatted you up the whole time we checked out and was still trying to talk to you as we went out the door."

Pierce pulled some fresh vegetables from the fridge and began washing them. "Sounds like you're going to have to go make one of these lovely ladies a grandma, Dad."

Rick shook his head, waving off their comments, but he was smiling. "For your information, the only girl who has my heart is this little one right here. Isn't that right, Ruby? Grandpa just wants to be here with his family. I want to spend my free time with you guys."

Ruby gurgled happily at him.

"Exactly," Rick agreed. "And as for the job, working as a regular firefighter instead of the chief is actually kind of like a partial retirement. I get to do all the fun stuff instead of sitting in the office, filling out paperwork and making schedules. There are times when I wonder if I did Hayden a disservice by leaving that burden to him."

"No," Pierce said as he brought the chopped veggies to the table. "I was just on the phone with him yesterday, and I almost couldn't get him to talk about anything else. He's always enjoyed being on the department, but this just might be the role he was destined for the whole time."

Holly scooped the meat onto a platter and brought it to the table, smiling. Fate had brought her and Pierce together. Once they'd found a way to make their relationship work, everything else seemed to fall into place—not just for the two of them but for everyone else. Rick was invigorated by the salty air, the abundance of ways to spend his time, and the chance to care for Ruby. Hayden was no longer surrounded by his immediate family, but he'd stepped into his own as fire chief for the Eugene-Springfield Fire Department. The photo Holly had dug from the ashes of the Westbrook house now lived in a new frame on their mantel, a reminder of the past.

Even Dylan seemed to enjoy the new friendships he'd formed with Pierce and Rick, and she loved having him over more often. At least she knew he wasn't dining alone while he waited for the chance to meet his mate. "Are you joining us, Dylan?"

"The way that smells, I don't think I can say no." He washed his hands and took a seat at the table.

As they all got settled, Ruby let out a loud squeal. The baby shook as dark fur burst out all over her skin. Her tiny baby fingers turned into long claws and she shook her head as her muzzle formed. She let out a shriek again, although it sounded much different now, coming from her bear form.

Rick laughed as he moved her around in his

arms to help accommodate the baby's new physique, and Ruby smacked her paws on the edge of the table. "I guess I'm not the only one you can't take to the grocery store. She's been doing that more and more often!"

"A perfect little cub," Dylan said with admiration. "I'm impressed that she can do that so early and with so much ease. You won't have to teach her how to shift at all."

"Just that she can't do it in public," Pierce noted. "She's got some very strong shifting genes in her."

"She does." Holly had been making a sandwich for Rick since his hands were full, but she stopped to admire her baby girl. Life had changed so much for her over the past year, and it was better than she ever could've imagined. Pierce's job meant that he was often gone at odd hours, and her own job occasionally took her away from home to research an assignment. They couldn't always be together as much as she would like, but they were truly making it work. When she'd visited Eugene, she knew there was a home she wanted desperately to come back to. Holly had even felt a bit selfish in telling Pierce she wouldn't stay in Oregon with him, but now she knew it was all for a good reason. This home—the one they'd created there together—was exactly what she'd craved in life. She not only had family surrounding her and a wonderful mate at her side, but an adorable baby girl.

Ruby let out her funny little squeal again. It was usually a sign that she was going to shift back into being a human baby, but not this time. Her body changed, but not into pink cheeks and chubby little toes. Her ears went from round to pointed. The deep brown on her muzzle changed to gray, and her body grew more lean and lanky. Her claws shrank, and her next squeal came out as a yip.

"Whoa! That's quite a tail there!" Rick exclaimed as he held onto the wolf pup.

Dylan dropped his fork. "I didn't know she could do that!"

"Neither did we," Holly admitted.

Pierce caught her eye from across the table. "I guess she's just like her mother."

She smiled at him and returned to her dinner, still in awe that such a young child would be capable of something like that. Pierce was right, though. Ruby was just like her. It was strange and magical to be both a wolf and a bear now that Pierce had marked her. She was still getting used to having two beasts inside her, but it was work she was willing to do.

When they'd finished dinner and cleared their plates, Dylan thanked them and headed back home. Holly saw him to the door, and when she turned back around, Pierce was watching her. "What?" she asked with a laugh.

"Well, the way Dad's been talking about it, I thought maybe you and I should take a run on the beach.

"I'll stay with Ruby," Rick offered. The infant was already asleep in his arms as he rocked her in front of the television. "I can handle her no matter what kind of animal she wants to be."

"Are you sure?" Holly asked.

"Go on," he urged, shooing them toward the door. "Get out of here."

Pierce took her hand as they stepped out the back door and ran down the sandy pathway to the beach. The Brigham clan owned most of the houses along this stretch of the Cape Cod Bay in Truro, meaning they didn't have to worry about being seen.

As they reached the flat of the beach, Holly let out her wolf. She stumbled a bit on her long, gangly legs and balanced herself with her tail. She felt strong and mighty as a bear, but her wolf felt light and free.

That was much better, Pierce commended her as they trotted along, just on the edge of the surf. *You're getting good.*

I'll have to catch up with Ruby, she cracked, still amazed by what their little girl could do. *She's going to grow up to be something special.*

She already is. Pierce slowed, sitting at the water's edge. *Just like you.*

Holly joined him, inhaling the salty air and soaking in the very last rays of the sun just before it slipped past the horizon. She leaned against Pierce, enjoying the feeling of his fur against hers. Looking out over the bay with her mate at her side, she never would've imagined experiencing all this when she'd gone to Eugene. It was an adventure she'd written about several times, but only in her private files.

It was the story of the century, but she wouldn't share it with anyone.

THE END

Thank you for reading *Wolf's Midlife Baby*!

Follow my next series for more midlife adventures with Dylan and the Brigham clan in Cape Cod. Read on for a preview of Destined Over Forty's first book, *Next Door Midlife Alpha.*

DYLAN

"You've got to be kidding me, Nina." Stacey Williams had just opened an email attachment on her cell phone and gaped at the flashy colors. "Why is this red?" She was relieved that even though she was technically on vacation, she'd made everyone run their marketing proposals by her before they went out to their clients.

"Because it looks good," Nina replied, already starting to sound anxious. "I thought it was bright and crisp, really eye-catching, you know?"

"Sure, but McKnight Insurance's main competitor already uses red in every piece of their marketing. We need to make sure McKnight stands out." Stacey rose from the desk in her home office, rubbing her forehead. She hadn't taken vacation time in over two years, skipping out for only a few hours when Vivian had a dance recital, and so far, this week wasn't feeling like much of a vacation at all. The thumping music coming from the first floor wasn't helping. She turned toward the stairs.

"But they use that knight as their logo to go along with their name, and the plume in his helmet is red," Nina protested.

"It's called a hackle." Not that the correct terminology mattered here, but she knew her client was particular about those kinds of details. She'd already spent an hour haggling with the graphic design department to make sure the little feather in the knight's helmet was waving in the wind in just the right manner. It was a good thing McKnight Insurance was paying them well, but Stacey knew they had to justify that fee. "If you use red for the background of everything else, the hackle won't stand out. We need to go with the blue we discussed."

Nina let out a long sigh. "I guess I can change it, but couldn't we see what the client thinks first? What if he really likes the red? And what is that noise?"

That was precisely what Stacey was trying to find out as she descended the last stair and looked into the living room where the painters were busy working. Apparently, they'd brought speakers loud enough to use at a music festival. "I said we're using blue."

"What?" Nina asked. "I can't hear you."

Aggravated with how this whole day was going, Stacey yelled, "I said we're using blue!"

The music stopped, and four painters suddenly turned to her. Gary, the one who seemed to be in charge, thumbed over his shoulder at the wall they'd just finished painting a soft shade of sage green. "No one said anything about blue. This was the paint sample Edgar gave me."

"Not you." Stacey pressed her hand to her forehead. "Nina, send me the new files when you finish them, and under no circumstance should you show anything to Mr. McKnight until I've seen them. I'll talk to you later."

Gary chuckled as he realized what had happened. "For a second there, I thought you were about to pound me into these old hardwood floors of yours. I'm glad I'm not the one who chose the wrong color if you're that mad."

"I'm not mad," she countered.

A few of the guys exchanged a look, and Stacey took a breath. "All right, maybe I am a little mad. But I should be able to take some time off work to get my house in order without worrying about coworkers messing everything up. I worked long and hard to get my job."

"I'm sure you did, or you wouldn't have been able to buy a house like this," Gary replied, gesturing around him at the high ceilings, gleaming hardwood floors, and arched doorways.

"The thing is, I need to get back to work. That's actually why I'm down here. I can appreciate that you want music playing, but could you keep it to a minimum? I can hear it all the way up in my office and can't concentrate." She didn't want to sound too irate, but these guys were working in her home.

"No problem, we're clocking out for the day, anyway." Gary put the lid on a bucket of paint and hammered it shut with a mallet.

"What?" Stacey checked her watch, shocked to see it was already five o'clock.

"Yep," Gary confirmed as he wrapped up his brushes and kicked the paint tarp out of the way. "We'll see you tomorrow, bright and early."

"Right." When they were out the back door and had headed down the road, Stacey realized just how tired she was. So much for time off. Didn't people go to the beach or mountains? It sounded nice, but Stacey knew she didn't have time. She slumped down onto the couch in the living room, which had been covered with a drop cloth.

She stared at the half-painted wall. The sage green contrasted horribly with the deep mustard yellow the previous owners had chosen. It wasn't cheap to have the place professionally painted, nor had it been cheap to have all the hardwood restored and the kitchen cabinets refinished. It meant Stacey had to continue to work all the harder at Martin Marketing, one of the biggest firms on the East Coast. But she was providing her children with the lifestyle they deserved, one where they had a spacious home to bring their friends to and a sprawling backyard to play in.

"And one with a big green stain on the ceiling," she muttered as she leaned back on the sofa and looked up. Someone had gotten sloppy with the sage paint and left a splotch on the freshly painted cream ceiling. Stacey stared at it for a minute, gritting her teeth. How could people be so careless? She would never get away with a mistake like that at her job. In fact, she'd seen people get fired for lesser offenses.

She checked her watch again. Stacey had made the mistake of getting a fitness tracker, even though she hardly had time to work out. It showed that her heart rate was steadily ticking upward—annoying thing. Todd would be dropping the kids off soon. Then, it would be time for a homemade dinner, baths, and a few snuggles before bedtime. She'd have to order a new pair of dance shoes for Vivian and schedule a haircut for Elijah, who seemed to go from neat and trim to caveman in a matter of a week. Oh, and she needed them to finalize the paint colors for their rooms and pick out new bedding.

Despite the growing list in her mind, Stacey couldn't stop staring at that green spot on the ceiling. "The painters will get it tomorrow," she told herself as she went into the kitchen to check the freezer and see what she could throw together once the kids got home. She knew Todd fed them nothing but fast food and chips, so she'd have to find something to balance it out. But as she crumbled tofu into a skillet, she couldn't stop thinking about that stupid green spot.

Stacey marched back into the living room and glared at it. It was just a bit of paint. It shouldn't matter, yet she knew she wouldn't get a damn thing done until it was gone. It was more offensive than the hideous yellow still waiting to be covered.

Well, fine. She was a capable woman. Gary had left his ladder there, and she moved it directly under the irritating green spot. Stacey checked the paint colors on the tops of the buckets and found the creamy color she'd chosen for the ceiling. Grabbing a flathead screwdriver, she stuck it under the lid and began prying it up. It wasn't working. She adjusted her grip and tried again, wondering how the hell these burly guys managed to shut the damn things so tight. With a final pop, the lid jumped off the bucket and landed on the floor. Paint side down.

"Seriously?" Stacey carefully lifted it, wondering just how much damage she'd done. Only a tiny dot of cream stained the deep honey of the hardwood since most of the liquid on the underside of the lid had already dried. Well, at least one thing was going her way.

She allowed herself a small moment of satisfaction as she found a clean brush and dipped it into the paint. There was something pleasing about it, a visual and tactile feeling she hadn't stopped to experience in a long time. Life was too busy for that. Swiping it on the edge of the bucket, she headed up the ladder.

When she reached the top, she realized she wasn't as close to that section of ceiling as she thought. No problem. Stacey reached out, swiping the dreamy cream over the green and trying not to be annoyed at her new paint color just because it was in the wrong place.

The ladder wobbled beneath her. Stacey braced her feet, getting it straight again. She'd have to be more careful, but she was almost done. She reached out for one last swipe with the brush, and the ladder tilted so softly under her that she didn't realize what was happening.

Until she found herself plummeting toward the floor. *No! No! No!* her mind cried out as her precious hardwood floor came barreling toward her. Her heart clenched. Her arms flailed. Her stomach clutched around her spine. A crack sounded through her brain and shuddered down her body as the world disappeared around her.

Stacey slowly opened her eyes. Her body felt strange as she pushed herself up off the floor. Her head spun as she got to her feet, but she was all right. That was a close one. The ladder was on its side, and as she moved toward it, her foot missed the floor.

Blinking, Stacey looked down. Neither of her feet was on the floor. The stunning hardwood she'd been so proud of was drifting further and further away as she floated up toward the very ceiling she'd been trying to paint. She studied the pitiful, sprawled form on the floor beneath her, realizing it was *her*. How could that be?

Something bright shone above her, but the ceiling was no longer there when she looked up. Warmth spread through her, and Stacey felt an overwhelming sense of unconditional love radiating from that brightness. Where was it coming from? For once, her mind was calm. She didn't understand, but she didn't need to. She let herself continue to rise, leaving everything else behind.

The glorious light began to shift, coalescing into a grassy green lawn with wildflowers swaying in the breeze. A fluffy white dog galloped up to her, his eyes bright and his tongue lolling.

"Tricky?" Stacey hadn't seen Tricky in years, not since she was a little girl. They used to play outside for hours, and her mind stumbled. Wasn't Tricky gone?

The dog wagged his tail and stomped his paws before turning back the way he'd come, and then he returned to Stacey to repeat the little show.

"All right, boy. I'll come with you. Is our fort still there?"

But Tricky didn't lead her to the makeshift fort Stacey had created all those years ago by throwing a blanket over the slide at the end of the swing set. He trotted happily in front of her until he was swirling around the legs of a man, tall and handsome with deep green eyes and a wide smile. He spread his arms out wide. "Come here, Gumdrop."

"Daddy?" Stacey fell into his arms, tears slipping from her eyes as she felt his embrace. It'd been so long, and she'd missed him so much. A cloudy fog had settled over her mind, and she still didn't quite understand what was happening. "Where have you been?"

"Here." He swept one arm out wide to encompass their parklike surroundings of green trees and brilliant flowers.

"It's beautiful." She moved back from her father just enough to bend down and touch the petals of a bright pink peony. It looked just like the ones that grew outside her first apartment.

"Yes, it is," her father agreed. "It always is, and the flowers bloom all the time."

"I like it." Stacey's body felt so good and relaxed. Her usual tension knots weren't making her bunch up her shoulders, and she couldn't think of anything she needed to do other than exist. "A lot."

"There's nothing more I'd like than to have you here with me," he replied, taking her hand, "but you've come too early."

"What? What do you mean?" Her father was there, and so was Tricky. Time didn't seem like it mattered at all.

"There are people who rely on you, people who need you more than anything. Some you know, and some you have yet to meet. You might be happy here, but they'd be lost without you." His brows scrunched with sympathy, the way they used to do when she went to him with a scraped knee or a broken heart.

Stacey immediately thought of her children. Vivian was always so bright and excitable. Elijah was quieter and incredibly smart. Then there was her mother. The two of them had been so close over the recent years. Her heart suddenly yearned for those who weren't there with her, and she understood. "I have to go back."

"You do," he confirmed, "but it was so wonderful to see you."

"You too, Dad. Will I see you again?" She hugged him, pulling him close and inhaling the scent of his cologne. She missed him so much, and though she couldn't quite put her thoughts in order, she knew she was about to miss him again.

"Eventually," he promised. "I've got something for you before you go." He held out his hand, and in his palm sat a small statue of a black bear. It sat up strong on its haunches with its nose in the air, looking up toward something. The glaze was glossy and smooth, and the soft eyes that'd been set into it were perfect. As she gazed at the bear, the feeling of unconditional love surrounding her blossomed in her heart, radiating in all directions.

"What...what's this?" Stacey reached out her hand to grasp it but missed.

"Don't worry, Gumdrop. You'll meet him again soon enough."

"What?" She tried again, but her father's hand was growing further and further away. Something was dragging her backward. Stacey cried and reached out, but her father waved goodbye. Wind rushed past her ears as she fell, tumbling down for an eternity. The entire weight of her existence landed on her when she hit the bottom.

A steady beeping sounded in her ears. She wanted someone to turn it off but couldn't make her lips or tongue work right in order to ask. Pain washed over her, shooting through every bone in her body and pulsing in her skull. It turned her stomach. Bright light still washed over her, but it wasn't the soft, gentle glow she'd experienced a few moments earlier. It was a harsh illumination that made her squint. She opened her eyes to see what it was, knowing Tricky was no longer there with her. Neither was her father.

"Mommy!" Two little arms wrapped around her.

Someone elbowed her on the other side, followed by more arms and hands. "Mommy's awake!"

"Nurse! Nurse!" A familiar voice called, and then her mother's face appeared before her. "Stacey! Oh, honey. I'm so glad you're back with us."

Me, too. She couldn't say it, not out loud, but when she looked down and saw both of her children clinging to her, she knew she meant it.

The nurse rushed in, checking her vitals and testing her reactions. Stacey lay there and went through the motions as best she could, but her eyes were on her mother and two children, where they'd retreated to the corner of the room to stay out of the nurse's way. Vivian had tears clinging to her lashes. Elijah's frown was so deep it looked like it might be permanent. They needed her so badly.

At that moment, she knew everything had to change.

———

ALSO BY MEG RIPLEY
ALL AVAILABLE ON AMAZON

Shifter Nation Universe

Mates Under the Mistletoe: A Shifter Nation Christmas Collection

Marked Over Forty Series

Fated Over Forty Series

Wild Frontier Shifters Series

Special Ops Shifters: L.A. Force Series

Special Ops Shifters: Dallas Force Series

Special Ops Shifters Series (original D.C. Force)

Werebears of Acadia Series

Werebears of the Everglades Series

Werebears of Glacier Bay Series

Werebears of Big Bend Series

Dragons of Charok Universe

Daddy Dragon Guardians Series

Shifters Between Worlds Series

Dragon Mates: The Complete Dragons of Charok Universe

Collection (Includes Daddy Dragon Guardians and Shifters Between Worlds)

More Shifter Romance Series

Beverly Hills Dragons Series

Dragons of Sin City Series

Dragons of the Darkblood Secret Society Series

Packs of the Pacific Northwest Series

Compilations

Forever Fated Mates Collection

Shifter Daddies Collection

Early Novellas

Mated By The Dragon Boss

Claimed By The Werebears of Green Tree

Bearer of Secrets

Rogue Wolf

ABOUT THE AUTHOR

Steamy shifter romance author Meg Ripley is a Seattle native who's relocated to New England. She can often be found whipping up her next tale curled up in a local coffee house with a cappuccino and her laptop.

Download *Alpha's Midlife Baby,* the steamy prequel to Meg's Fated Over Forty series, when you sign up for the Meg Ripley Insiders newsletter!

Sign up by visiting www.authormegripley.com

<u>Connect with Meg</u>

amazon.com/Meg-Ripley/e/B00Z8I9AXW
tiktok.com/@authormegripley
facebook.com/authormegripley
instagram.com/megripleybooks
bookbub.com/authors/meg-ripley
goodreads.com/megripley
pinterest.com/authormegripley